SYSTEMA PARADOXA

ACCOUNTS OF CRYPTOZOOLOGICAL IMPORT

VOLUME 25
SNAPPED UP
A TALE OF THE BEAST OF BUSCO

AS ACCOUNTED BY AARON ROSENBERG
ILLUSTRATED BY JW HARP

NEOPARADOXA
Pennsville, NJ
2025

PUBLISHED BY
NeoParadoxa
A division of eSpec Books
PO Box 242
Pennsville, NJ 08070
www.especbooks.com

ISBN: 978-1-956463-79-8
ISBN (ebook): 978-1-956463-78-1

Interior Design: Danielle McPhail
www.sidhenadaire.com

Cover Art: JW Harp
Cover Design: Mike and Danielle McPhail, McP Digital Graphics
Interior Illustration: JW Harp

Copyediting: Greg Schauer and John L. French

Dedication

For Jenifer, Adara, and Arthur.
Who deserve to be celebrated like Oscar.

Author's Note

The people named in this book are not real, and any resemblance to real people is entirely coincidental.

The historical figures named herein were real.

The town of Churubusco, Indiana is very real, as are all the buildings and businesses mentioned.

Turtle Days is also very real and has been running for over seventy years.

As for Oscar… well, you'll just have to decide for yourself.

CHAPTER ONE

Rob looked up from his cell phone and sighed. "Tell me again why we had to get here a day early?" He hated that his voice rose to a whine at the end of that, but he was hot, sweaty, and tired. There'd been more traffic on the road than they'd expected, so it had taken longer to get here from Chicago, and the car's AC was still on the fritz. Plus, as usual, this place's Wi-Fi sucked. At least there was a bit of a breeze up here on the hill!

Jeannie glanced at him over her shoulder, tossed her long blonde hair back, and laughed. "Stop being such a baby," she teased. "I've almost got this set up." She was the more outdoorsy of them, and Rob had learned long ago to let her handle things like the tent. Which was fine by him, except that he felt a bit useless at the moment. Especially since he had no signal and couldn't even surf the web or stream any music.

"There!" She straightened and stepped back, arms crossed. "See?" Sure enough, their reliable old tent stood there, sturdy as always. "Grab the air mattress."

"Yes, ma'am." He picked the bundle up and carried it into the tent, then used the electric pump to inflate it, his mood lifting with the mattress top. By the time it was full, he was smiling once more.

His wife noticed the improvement at once, and laughed again, throwing her arms around his neck. "Feeling better?" She kissed him and he responded eagerly.

"I am now." The sun was nearly down, shadows stealing across the rise, and with the dark came a welcome dip in the mid-June heat.

"Look." She nudged him and he twisted about, an arm around her waist. Together they gazed out over the campground, and to the lake beyond. "See? If we'd come tomorrow, we wouldn't have been able to grab such a good spot."

"Yeah, yeah. You're right." At an elbow from her, he quickly added, "Like always."

She turned to reward that with a kiss but stopped as a strange sound rose from beyond. Something like a hiss, mixed with odd, harsh clicks.

"What's that?" They both peered about in the thickening gloom, but there were only a few vehicles parked down below, and no other tents nearby.

Still the sounds continued.

"There!" Jeannie grabbed his arm, pointing with her other hand. Rob followed her gesture — and froze.

Because rising from the lake down below was an enormous shape that could only be a head. But what a head! Even from here they could tell that it was ridged or scaled like some sort of reptile, with a sharply curved mouth almost like a bird beak and bright, round eyes.

Given where they were, there was only one thing it could be.

"Oscar," Rob breathed, and his wife nodded enthusiastically, her grip on his arm tightening with excitement. The head disappeared back below the lake's surface with a loud splash, and the couple exchanged gleeful grins, though Rob wished he'd thought to snap a photo.

After all, they'd just seen the fabled Beast of Busco!

CHAPTER TWO

Andy Shah leaned forward, wedging himself into the space between the Sienna's front seats. "Yo," he said, placing a hand on Mateo's shoulder. "Bro. We don't stop soon, I'm gonna pee all over these back seats. And trust me, my uncle wouldn't be too happy about that."

"Never mind your uncle," Olivia "Vi" Landry offered from the seat beside his. "*I* wouldn't be happy with it! Besides, with your aim you're liable to hit *me*, along with everything else in sight."

Twisting around, Andy tossed a stray candy at his seatmate. It went wide and bounced off the minivan's side door instead. "See?"

"All I'm saying," Andy continued, returning to his plea, "Is that it's about time for a break, yeah? Stretch our legs, get some food that isn't pre-wrapped, maybe even find beds for the night."

Nia Carr nodded. "I'm with Andy," she said, her voice low and melodic as ever. "We've been on the road all day. Time to find some place to hole up for the night." She grimaced up at the sky, which was slate gray. "And try to avoid any more rain, if we can." They'd already had to drive through a downpour and had seen signs for at least one road being washed out.

Mateo Diaz, who was currently on driving duty, grunted. "Yeah, okay, fine," he said finally. A sign was approaching, and he squinted at it. "Churubusco, one mile," he read. "We'll stop there."

Satisfied, Andy slid back to his place. "Cool. Thanks, bro." He frowned. "What the hell's a Churubusco, anyway? Are we still in Pennsylvania?"

That made Vi laugh. "You slept through half of that and all of Ohio, you goof," they teased. "And most of the storm that covered it. We're in Indiana already." Their dark eyes shone with good humor from behind their glasses, and Andy laughed along with them. It was hard to take offense at Vi's verbal jabs.

Mateo took the exit ramp with smooth expertise, guiding the minivan off the highway. A sign appeared ahead of them, straddling the road: "Welcome to Churubusco," Nia read off. "Turtle Town, USA." A cartoon of a turtle wearing a sailor hat adorned the sign next to the wording. "O-kay."

"Guess they really like turtles here?" Andy offered. "Turtle soup? Turtlenecks? Ooh, maybe those chocolate-and-caramel ones! Those're turtles, right?"

Mateo smirked. "Yeah, if my chocolate comes with a little sailor hat, I'm not eating it."

The road narrowed, and a handful of homes and businesses sprang up around them. "So how far to this town?" Andy asked.

Vi laughed again. "I think we're in it."

The others all stared, but Vi had grown up in rural Minnesota. If any of them knew anything about small towns, it was them.

"The Farmers and Merchants Bank?" Nia muttered. "You must be joking."

"Club Ideal Fish and Game," Andy read off the next sign. "Integrity Meats. Hey, I like my food to have moral fiber—or some kinda fiber, anyways! Oh, the Dollar General! I'd always wondered how much it cost to make general. My parents'd be so proud."

But Mateo had been watching for other things, and now he smiled, hitting the turn indicator. "Ah, civilization at last," he quipped as he pulled into the parking lot of a Subway.

None of them were in any mood to argue. At least they knew Subway could accommodate their varied food requirements! Andy was throwing open his door almost before they'd stopped, slipping out sideways and turning his near-fall into a cartwheel. "Woo-hoo! Solid ground!"

"It isn't like we were flying at ten thousand feet," Nia reminded him, but was too busy stretching to put any venom into the remark. It was already a long way from New York, after all, and they all took a minute to shake out their limbs before traipsing toward the sandwich shop.

Inside, all four of them relaxed, soothed by the familiar interior. It was mostly empty and the quartet quickly ordered and collected their sandwiches, chips, and drinks, claiming a table right by the front window.

"Ah, so good," Vi exclaimed, taking a big bite of their veggie sub.

"It'd be better with some turkey or ham or beef on it," Andy suggested, and received a potato chip to the forehead for his troubles. "Thanks, don't mind if I do." He quickly popped that into his mouth. The action provoked a response from the only other group there, a trio of teens in the back corner, but with the ease of long practice the foursome ignored them.

"Quiet place," Nia commented as they finished their food. "Think there's a hotel anywhere nearby?"

Mateo shrugged. "Dunno. Doesn't hurt to ask, I guess. At least if there is, we might be able to afford it." They were all college students and thus traveling on a limited budget, after all.

Rising easily to his feet, he headed back to the counter, ignoring the teens, who turned to watch. "Hi, sorry," he started, smiling at the girl there who'd rung them up. "Is there a hotel around here?"

She nodded, patting her sleek dark hair and returning his smile, though that quickly turned to a frown. "Uh, yeah, there is—but they're probably full up." She pointed at a poster on the wall behind her.

"Turtle Days?" He read. "What's that?" He noted that, whatever it was, the event ran for four days—and had just started today.

"Oh, it's awesome!" The girl, whose name tag proclaimed her as Cindy, told him. "It's our biggest festival of the year! All about our very own monster, the Beast of Busco!" That produced a snort from the local onlookers.

Her voice carried to Mateo's friends, though, and they all rose and wandered over to join the conversation. "What's a Beast of Busco?" Vi asked, eyes bright with curiosity. "I've never heard of it." And that was saying something, considering how much they read!

"Well, its proper name is Oscar, after the man who first saw it," Cindy confided, "but most people just call it the Beast. It's an alligator snapping turtle." She grinned. "Only, it's the size of a Prius."

The foursome stared at her. "A turtle… the size of a small car?" Andy repeated. "That seems… unlikely."

His skepticism only fueled their server's enthusiasm. "I know, right? They can get big, snapping turtles, but not that big! Leastways, not normally. But Oscar's been around over a hundred years, and they keep growing." She pointed out of the shop and to the left. "In the town square there's a statue of him. Only, it ain't life-sized."

Nia was absorbing all of this with her usual poise. "So it's an urban legend," she concluded. "Like the Jersey Devil, or the Mothman, or the Wunk. And you hold a festival every year celebrating it." Which made sense, if it was this town's only claim to fame.

Cindy nodded. "Yep! Lots of places here in Indiana have folk tales and local legends, like the Reno Gang's buried treasure down in Floyd and Jackson Counties, or Jim Genna's gangster stash near here in Marshall County. Ours is Oscar. We've got live music, games, rides, talent shows, cookouts, crafts, all sorts of stuff! And Saturday to end it all there's a parade, fireworks and a big laser light show!"

Mateo was looking at his friends. "That does sound like fun," he agreed. "Only, you said all the hotels are full up already?"

"Oh, yeah," Cindy answered. "People come from miles around for this. Even out of state." She thought a second. "You could head over to Blue Lake or Tippecanoe, though. They're just outside town, and there's campgrounds there. Hookups if you've got an RV, space if you've got a tent. Blue Lake's even got a few cabins you can rent."

He nodded. "That might work just fine, provided the rain's stopped." Vi had insisted they pack a tent and sleeping bags, just in case, though the other three had no idea how to even put one together. Still, that would almost certainly be budget-friendly. "And staying for the festival could be fun. Who knows, maybe we'll even see this Beast for ourselves."

Cindy laughed. "Yeah, good luck with that. Last sighting was in the late Forties. But y'all should definitely stay. It's a hoot." Her eyes were entirely on Mateo as she said this, and her smile was inviting.

The other three drifted away. They gathered their trash, deposited it, and headed outside, letting Mateo work his usual charm as he and the server exchanged numbers.

The fast-food place's door had barely shut behind them before it swung open again. But it wasn't Mateo who emerged. Instead it was the three teens who'd been laughing and snorting at them from their corner.

"You don't really believe all that, do ya?" one of them demanded, deliberately stepping into Vi's personal space and glowering down at them from behind a mop of red hair. "All that BS about Oscar? As if!" He followed the comment with a deliberate stare and a sneer. "And what're you supposed ta be, anyway?" His two friends laughed along with him.

Vi glared right back at him. "Me?" They batted their eyelashes and leaned in, making him reel back in confusion—just as their foot hooked his leg, knocking him off balance. He flailed, but only one of the others' quick intervention saved him from toppling off the curb. Vi just grinned. "I'm complicated."

"Why, you little—" the teen started to charge them, fists balled, but Nia slid into his path. "Move it, missy."

Nia shrugged. "Okay." And, seizing his hand and side, she spun him around, twirling him before releasing him to slam into the shop's wall. "Whoops. Not too light on your feet, are you?"

One of the teen's friends had had enough. "I'll show you!" he shouted, launching himself in their direction—only to have Andy cartwheel forward, his feet catching their attacker square in the chin. The boy staggered back, bumping into his two friends just as the door opened again and Mateo emerged.

"Problem?" he asked, raising an eyebrow.

Outnumbered and clearly outclassed, the three locals backed away, then scrambled across the parking lot, piling into a beat-up pickup that might have been black at one point. Tires squealing, they peeled out of the lot, making rude gestures as they drove away.

"Amateurs," Nia sneered, watching them go. Then she doubled over, laughing. "Oh, man! Did you see their faces when I spun the one?"

"Or what about when Vi tripped his buddy?" Andy asked, fist-bumping them. "Nice one! Don't mess with the drama kids, am I right?"

Mateo shook his head, though he was chuckling with the rest of them. "Yeah, yeah. I leave you alone for two minutes…"

"More like we left you alone," Andy pointed out, grinning. "And how'd that work out, Romeo?" he asked, punching Mateo in the shoulder. "This gonna happen every time we stop?"

Mateo just grinned. "What can I say? I'm irresistible."

"I think you mean incorrigible," Vi suggested. "Or unbelievable." The other two giggled.

"Irritable?" Nia offered. "No, wait, that's us at your behavior."

"Irrational?" was Andy's contribution. "For caring about stuff like that in the first place?"

"Just 'cause you don't understand it," Mateo countered, "doesn't make it wrong." Vi and Nia both nodded—on that topic, at least, Andy was the odd man out. But they did their best not to make him feel pressured about it. They all had their own take on things. It was part of what had brought them together in the first place.

"Anyway, the festival could be fun to check out," Vi said, bringing the conversation back to safer ground. "And it might be nice to stay in one place and chill for a day or two. We're not in any rush, right?"

Andy nodded. "Yeah, we gotta get the car to its new owner within two weeks," he reminded. "But long as we do that, we're all good."

"It is still a ways to LA," Mateo pointed out. "Especially if we're stopping in Chicago" — with a nod to Nia, who was from there — "or Minnesota." That was to Vi. "Still, we've got some time." He laughed. "And I've always wanted to see a turtle the size of a car!"

"Not me!" Andy protested, waving his hands. "I like my reptiles carry-sized!" He was in the minority there, however, and without an official vote it had clearly been decided.

They were going to stay and scope this "Turtle Days" event out.

Chapter Three

Back in the minivan, they had a quick discussion, though it was mostly one-sided:

Mateo: "So, we going downtown to see what's what?"

Nia: nodding

Vi: nodding

Andy, with a groan: "Fine, whatever."

With that decided, Mateo backed the car out of the lot and aimed it north, the way Cindy had pointed. It took only a few minutes and passing a handful of streets before they reached an intersection larger than any of the previous ones.

"East State Road and North Main Street," Nia commented, reading the street signs. "Quaint." She laughed when Vi slapped her shoulder. "Okay, okay. Sorry!"

Andy was leaning forward again, staring out the front window. "So," he asked, stabbing his hand forward. "You think that's this giant monster she told us about?"

They all looked. There on the corner, right in front of an H&R Block, was a statue — of a Native American man with a full headdress.

"Funny," muttered Mateo, who was as dark as the bronzed figure. Nia, who was even darker, grunted agreement.

But their friend scoffed. "Not him," he insisted. "Dude. There." And his hand dipped a little lower.

Squinting, the others saw it. In front of the statue was a second sculpture, this one much lower to the ground. It was simply shaped, with very little detail beyond rough yellow blocks on the back for its shell and indented circles for its eyes, but it was four-legged, green, and slightly hump-backed.

Just like a crude rendition of a turtle.

"Doesn't look all that imposing," Vi agreed. "And where is every-body? I thought she said this was a big deal."

The others shrugged—all except Nia, who rolled down her window. "Listen," she said, inclining her elegant head. They did, even Andy going still for a moment.

Which meant all of them could now hear the sounds of music.

"Follow that concert!" Vi ordered, giggling, and Mateo saluted, grinning, before taking them on down the road. That did bring them past the two statues, and Nia read off the taller one's plaque as they passed:

"Little Turtle. War Chief of the Miami Nation. 1752-1812."

Andy snickered. "So it's the Tale of Two Turtles?" That earned him a glare from Nia and a poke in the side from Vi, but he was too doubled over in laughter to care. Mateo shook his head but couldn't hold back a smile. Neither could the rest of them. Andy might be a goof at times, but he was *their* goof.

The sounds led them along Main Street until, through a gap in trees and houses on the left, they saw what looked like a park or a fairground. Whatever it was, it was wide, flat, covered in grass, and filled with people.

"Betting that's the place," Nia said, and Mateo took the next left. The road curved to the right, then left again, bringing them to a wide-open gate and a large sign proclaiming, "Welcome to Churubusco Community Park." Beyond that was complete chaos.

Mateo pulled into a spot along the side, slipping the Sienna neatly between a small hatchback and a massive pickup. "Right, time to go meet the locals, mingle, play some games, and maybe see an urban legend," he declared, hopping out.

The others followed, even Andy perking up at the idea of bright lights, fun activities, and snacks.

The Turtles Days festival certainly appeared to be in full swing as the foursome entered the crowd. Everywhere they looked there were activities, ranging from a tractor pull to a foot race to a car show to arts and crafts to classic carnival games. Most people were dressed normally, but here and there they saw folks sporting Turtle Days shirts or hats, and others with shirts showing a massive turtle. One of those bore a plain white nametag on its enormous shell, and Vi squinted to make out the lettering.

"Oscar?" they read. "Oh, that's right, it's—"

"Yep!" That was from the woman wearing said shirt, who didn't seem the least bit annoyed or embarrassed at the close study. "It's his name, after Oscar Fulk, who first spotted him in 1898." She held out her hand. "Howdy! Angie Wick, Turtle Days vice-president. Your first time with us?"

"Uh…" Vi awkwardly accepted the handshake. "Yeah. Came in from New York. Just passing through but saw the poster. Sounded neat."

"Oh, it is!" Angie was probably twice their age, big and blonde and, evidently, endlessly cheerful. "Four full days of fun! Y'all're more'n welcome!" She took Vi's arm and spun them both around in a lazy circle, pointing as they turned. "Concessions that way, games there, rides there, vendors there, contests there, crafts there, car show there, tractor pull there." From a back pocket she produced a folded paper map. "Here ya go. I know it's a lot." She winked. "Enjoy!" Then she'd been swallowed up by the crowd, which enthusiastically received her.

The others crowded round as Vi unfolded the map. "This thing is huge," Andy said, his tone half wonder and half glee. "Look, there's a BBQ cook-off!" He'd have vanished, too, if Nia's quick reflexes hadn't let her latch onto his arm and hold the lanky boy in place. "What? I'm starving!"

"We literally just ate," Vi pointed out, rolling their eyes, but got only a shrug in return. Not that it was any great surprise, really. After an entire semester together, they all knew how much Andy could pack away.

"Okay, we can look around a bit, but everybody stay close," Mateo warned. "Anybody gets separated, head back to the car. Right?" They all nodded, and Andy immediately took the lead, making a beeline for the barbecue. The others groaned but followed.

His destination proved to be a large tent whose one end was filled with checkered-tablecloth-covered tables. And on each one, stacked high, was mound upon mound of fresh barbeque.

"So, what?" Andy asked the tent as a whole. "We just grab a plate and load up?"

"Not quite," a tall, slim woman replied. Her dark skin and short dark hair went nicely with her tan and black uniform, and even in the tent's shade the star on her chest gleamed. "You buy a ticket over there, five dollars apiece. That gets you a tray and a scorecard. You load up the tray, try a little bit of everything, and rate them all. Hand in the empty tray and the full scorecard when you're done." Her smile was polite. "Got that?"

Andy gulped, peering up at her—he wasn't used to having to tilt his head back to see someone's eyes. "Ma'am, yes, ma'am!" And, glancing about, he quickly headed toward the line to one side, where a man and a woman were taking money and doling out trays and cards in return.

"Sorry about him," Mateo offered. "He eats like it's his life's work."

The officer nodded. "No problem. You folks new in town?" Her smile stayed the same, cool and distant. "Rhonda Cohn. Town marshal."

Mateo introduced himself, Nia, and Vi. "Yeah, just passing through," he admitted. "Hope that's okay."

"It is," he was assured. "Long as you don't cause any trouble."

"We won't," Nia promised. The marshal seemed to accept that, because with a nod she turned and sauntered off.

None of the rest of them were hungry, but when Andy emerged with a massive heap of food   they all found it in themselves to nibble some. Everything was excellent, and they were still polishing off the last few ribs—Vi had stuck with things like grilled mushrooms and braised cauliflower—when a couple sat down at the trestle table they'd claimed.

"Sorry, okay if we share?" the woman asked. She didn't look that much older than them.

"Sure, plenty of space," Mateo answered. He nodded at her shirt and the guy's, both of which were from previous Turtle Days. "You two locals, or just return customers?"

"The latter," the guy answered with a chuckle. "We're from Chicago. Been coming for five, six years now. Rob Porter. This is my wife, Jeannie." After introductions he asked, "What about you four?"

"First time," Nia told him. "I'm from Chicago, too, though. Enjoying it here so far."

"You have no idea!" Jeannie said, grinning. "We love it here—but this year's already been the best yet! Where're you staying?"

"We heard something about a lake nearby, with camping?" Vi replied. "Blue Lake?"

Rob nodded. "That's where we are! It's cool. I mean, seriously bare bones, and forget about cell service, but cool." He smiled. "Especially this year!"

He and his wife were laughing at some private joke, but evidently didn't want to share. They were friendly enough otherwise, though, and as the foursome rose Jeannie told them, "Hope to see you out there. And keep your eyes open—you never know what might be around!" That led to more giggling from the couple, which continued as Nia led the way out.

"That was odd," Vi commented once they were back outside. "Right?"

"Eh, country folk're weird," Andy said, twisting to avoid their swat. "Right, on to the games!"

Nobody argued. At least being in a crowd like this reminded them all of New York City, and their time together there. And hey, they were all theater kids. What could suit them better than a small-town carnival based around a mythical creature?

Vi had already decided that they would be picking up at least one tee-shirt before they hit the road again.

Chapter Four

By the time they left the fair, they were all exhausted.

"Whew!" Andy rubbed his stomach. "I think I'm actually full, for once!"

Nia snorted from her quickly-becoming-customary spot in the front passenger seat. "And to think," she called back, "all it took was a plate of barbeque, three corn dogs, two apple fritters, a bag of kettle corn, another of cotton candy, a turkey leg, a giant pickle, and a cheesecake on a stick."

"I know, right?" He grinned back at her, as usual unfazed by her sarcasm. "So, time to hit the hay? Or at least figure out where we're bedding down for the night?"

"Blue Lake Campground," Vi replied from next to him. They held up their phone. "It's ten minutes away. Head north, then turn left on East 550 North."

"So which is it?" Andy asked. "East, or north?" He laughed when they elbowed him, squirming to get away. "Hey, watch it! I'm like a piñata at the moment, only full of tasty food!"

"Do not hit him with a bat," Nia warned. "Much as you might like to."

They were still squabbling good-naturedly when Mateo turned off onto a smaller road — right beside a sign reading "Welcome to Blue Lake Campground."

"Found it!" he sang out. The others swatted him about the head and shoulders, but carefully, since he was driving.

A minute later he pulled into the visitor parking lot, snagging one of the last open spaces. "Popular place," Nia commented as they all climbed out of the minivan. "But I guess beggars can't be choosers."

"Great view," Vi noted, and the others followed their gaze past a handful of small buildings and a slew of campers and RVs to a handsome little lake beyond. The sun was just beginning to set, and its light filtered across the water, leaving trails of gold and peach and pale violet atop the shimmering blue water.

The nearest building had a sign proclaiming it the office and general store, so they headed there first. "Evening!" the man behind the counter exclaimed as they entered. "You folks looking to camp?"

"Unless you've got someplace with actual beds available," Nia said, but the man was already shaking his head.

"Sorry, cabins're already taken. Most a' the camper spots, too, and about half the hill." He leaned in a little. "Ain't ya heard? The Beast is back!"

The four friends exchanged glances. "The giant turtle?" Mateo finally asked.

"That's the one! Just got spotted out in the lake last night!" The man—his name tag read "Larry"—grinned. "Ain't it awesome?"

"Awesome," they all agreed, Andy with less enthusiasm than the others. "So, I guess we're camping." Only Vi looked excited about this news.

"You got it. And don't worry, we had all that rain last week, but it's been just a drizzle or two since, ground's plenty dry, and a bit more springy'n usual." Larry frowned in thought. "It's thirty a night for the tent, and that's supposed ta cover two adults and one kid. Then it's eight a night per person after that." He winked at them. "But I figure three is three, and none a' ya're all that old, so let's just go with the tent and one extra, for thirty-eight a night. If you're staying for the rest of the festival, that's three nights, so a hundred fourteen in all. How's that sound?"

Mateo smiled. "Sounds great. Thank you so much." Vi, who was in charge of their pooled travel money, pulled out some cash and paid the man, receiving a key and a parking pass in return.

"That's for the bath house," Larry told them, indicating the key. "It's only one per tent, sorry." He pulled out a map of the place. "You can pitch your tent anywhere up here," he continued, indicating an area slightly above them labeled "Primitive camping." "Bath house's right here behind the office. Snack machines're here, too, along the back. Gazebo down here's a nice spot to eat at but you can chow down anywhere, really, long as you clean up after yourself. Laundry's here if you need it, coin-operated. And we got snacks and such here in the office, too, even some real food for sale if you don't wanna use the machines."

"Thanks," Mateo said again. "I'm sure we'll be back around once we're settled."

Returning to the Sienna, they grabbed their bags and the camping equipment. But after they'd trudged along the road and up the hill, it was Vi who took charge.

"Find some branches for a fire," they instructed, selecting a spot for their campsite. "And rocks, fist-sized, to make a circle for it." They got to work setting up the tent itself, moving with practiced ease. The others stared a second, not used to this level of confidence or assertiveness from their quiet friend, but soon snapped out of it and got to their assigned tasks.

By the time they'd gathered the branches and made a ring of the rocks, Vi had the tent set up and sleeping bags laid out in a neat row within. Next they built a fire. Even though it had been warm during the day, there was a breeze up here on the hill, and the blaze provided some welcome warmth. Plus it just looked and smelled nice.

Once that was done, they traipsed back down to the store to see what they could find for dinner.

"Why is it," Andy asked, polishing off his fifth hot dog, "that food cooked over an open flame just tastes better?"

Nia shrugged, then burped, but delicately. "No idea, but you're not wrong."

The sun had gone down now, leaving them only their fire, similar glimmers from other campers, and the stars above for light. It was pleasantly cool, and the air smelled of pine needles, lake water, wood smoke, and cooked food. All of them were comfortably full and enjoying just sitting sprawled on the ground. For Mateo, Nia, and Andy, it was a rare occurrence being able to see so many stars, or simply looking across the horizon and not spying any buildings.

Then a strange sound like a loud, angry hiss burst forth, echoing all around them.

"What was that?" Andy asked, sitting bolt upright. "Somebody's balloon spring a leak?"

"I don't think that's a balloon, Andy," Mateo replied, as a series of sharp clicks broke through the hissing. "Some kind of animal, maybe?"

They heard movement nearby, and a handful of other people rushed out of the darkness. Two of them were the couple they'd met before, Rob and Jeannie Porter. Both of them were grinning like mad, though the others looked more confused and surprised. "Did you hear that?" Rob asked.

"Hard not to," Nia drawled as she and her friends stood. "What is it, exactly?"

Her fellow Chicagoans laughed. "It's the Beast!" Jeannie answered excitedly. "The Beast of Busco!"

"That's..." Vi started to say something but was cut off by more hisses and clicks. "It *does* sound like something's out there," they admitted finally, during a gap in the noises.

"Oh, it's out there," Rob assured them. "We saw it just last night, down on the lake! We're gonna go see if we can get a closer look!" And he and his wife headed down the hill, followed by the others they'd gathered.

The foursome watched them go. "Nuts," Andy proclaimed, shaking his head. "A turtle the size of a car? Even if it's real, why'd you wanna go toward it instead of running the other way? 'Specially if it's real! Can you imagine the kinda damage a thing like that could do to a handsome young thespian?" He struck a pose—only to deflate when Nia kicked him in the knee. "Hey!"

Surprisingly, it was Vi who shook their head. "I dunno," they said slowly. "If it *is* real—and I'm not saying it is—but if it *is*, it *would* be pretty cool to see."

"A once in a lifetime sight," Mateo agreed, grinning. "I'm in."

Nia shrugged. "Eh, sure, why not? Can't be any scarier than Times Square at rush hour!"

Andy opened his mouth to protest further but, seeing he was outnumbered, sighed. "Fine. But if it eats me, it's all your fault!"

"Don't worry," Nia promised him as they began following the path the Porters had left. "If that happens, we'll make sure the car still gets where it's going."

"Gee, thanks," Andy muttered. "You're all heart."

CHAPTER FIVE

The slope down the hill was mostly full, and they were forced to dodge tents of various sizes and shapes. "How'd they do that?" Andy asked as he nearly ran over one shaped like a perfect dome.

"Curved panels and flexible rods," Vi answered absently. "Looks cool, pops up all on its own—but a stiff wind'll blow it right over, and it's got no insulation at all." They shrugged. "Good for play tents in the backyard, not so much for the real outdoors."

The foursome kept going, but as they reached flat ground and crossed the dirt road there, leaving the tents behind, Andy stopped. "Smell that?" he said, lifting his head to sniff the air.

Warily, the others followed his actions. "What?" Nia asked after a second. "All I'm getting is the trees, the lake, the fires—and somebody's hot dogs."

But their skinny, perpetually hungry friend shook his head, his eyes bright. "Those aren't dogs," he whispered, a hint of adoration in his tone. "They're brauts!" And he plunged forward, disappearing among the rows of trailers and RVs between them and the lake.

"Andy!" Vi stamped their foot but gave up a second later with a sigh. "Typical."

Mateo and Nia both laughed. "Yeah, he's definitely ruled by his stomach," Nia agreed. "And it's a tyrant."

"Should we go find him?" Vi asked. But Mateo shrugged.

"He knows where the tent is, and it's not like even he can miss the hill," he pointed out. "Besides, I don't wanna miss a chance at seeing this Beast just because Andy got hungry. Again."

That decided them, and the trio took the path between the trailers, focused on the waters ahead and the creature potentially lurking within them.

After all, Vi thought as they trailed the other two, how much trouble could Andy really get into out here?

Andy was following his nose, which was a finely tuned instrument. Sure enough, it led him right to a trailer, one of those where you could extend an awning from the side. That had been set up over a grill, a folding table, and several chairs, and a couple were there, one tending the fire and the other sitting and enjoying a beer.

"Hi," Andy said, almost stumbling over them as he planted his feet. "Sorry, but that smell—wow!"

"Right?" the one at the fire replied with an easy smile. They were a little shorter than Andy, and a little wider, with close-cropped, sandy hair and a friendly, ruddy face. "Best brauts around. You want one?"

"Heck, yeah!" He grinned, holding out his hand. "I'm Andy."

"Tay," the griller replied, shaking. "And that's Rhet." The one at the table, who was even shorter but also slimmer and darker, nodded. "Have a seat, they're almost ready."

Andy laughed. "Don't mind if I do!" He plonked down, and soon found himself trading life stories with the pair, who were from Indianapolis. It was a good twenty minutes later before, having polished off two brauts and a beer, Andy rose and, with much thanks, took his leave.

"Sorry to eat and run," he told his hosts. "But my friends're probably wondering where I am. Thanks again, though. That was super, and not just the food."

"Our pleasure," Rhet assured him. "Come back any time. Bring your friends, too. The more the merrier."

"Will do," he promised. Two steps from the trailer's awning and the shadows swallowed him up again. Another two and he couldn't even see the trailer.

Four more, and he realized he wasn't sure which way the tent was.

"Well, if I hit the lake I've gone the wrong direction," he reasoned, and continued the way he was facing.

It was like traveling between giant boulders in the dead of night—there'd be nothing but darkness and then, suddenly, a big white or silver shape would rear up out of nowhere as another trailer swam into view. Andy found himself getting more and more turned around, and more and more concerned. Didn't any of these people believe in lights?

He'd just passed one trailer, as dark inside as the rest, when he heard a strange noise. Something like a hiss, followed by several clicks.

Whatever it was, it sounded big—and close by.

"That had better be somebody with a leaky balloon and tap shoes," Andy muttered to himself. He turned, stepping around another RV—

—and froze.

Because there, up ahead of him, was a strange, shadowy figure easily a foot taller than his own six-two, four-legged, hump-backed, and as wide as a small car.

"No. Way." Andy stared up at it. It stomped closer, but he couldn't move. Closer still. Even closer. Now he could make out the shape of its head, heavily scaled and flat across the top, eyes set to either side, with a lipless hooked mouth.

When it was only a few feet away, it opened that mouth—opened it wide—and screeched like an owl.

That was it. Andy took off running.

He slipped on the dirt and grass, nearly tumbled headfirst, but caught himself, turning the fall into a roll and putting that momentum into his escape. The thing behind him—it had to be the Beast, what else?—roared and came charging after, clicking and clattering as it went.

Nearing another RV, Andy grabbed hold of its driver-side mirror and used that to haul himself in a sharp turn around the vehicle's front. The tight space seemed to confound his pursuer, whose shell snagged on the mirror, bringing it to a hissing halt.

While it was trying to pull free, Andy sprinted for the next bit of shelter.

It was right behind him—how the hell did something that big move that fast?—and he swerved desperately to the left.

One foot hit a patch of mud and shot out from under him. Andy hit the ground hard.

Gasping for breath, he rolled to the side—right under an RV. The Beast bellowed its frustration.

Scuttling all the way across, Andy slid out and to his feet. *Time to go!*

He sprinted forward—and nearly slammed right into the thing as it rounded the corner. He'd never have believed something its size could maneuver like that.

Fortunately, it had no arms to grab him with. Andy ducked a lunging peck from the mouth and squirmed past. Then, not bothering to look back, he gathered himself and shot forward.

Dirt sprayed up as he charged across another road. He burst past a few more trailers, only noticing he could see them when he cleared the last one and found himself facing a smattering of buildings and some playground equipment.

He was back by the main office. Which meant he'd wound up going sideways instead of up.

That wasn't his biggest concern right now, however. Panting, Andy put his back against the office's wall, resisting the urge to slide down in a heap. No, if that thing closed in again, he had to be ready to run. Assuming his legs could manage. And his lungs. And his heart.

But a minute passed, and he saw no sign of pursuit. Nor did he hear any more clicking and hissing.

He waited another minute or two, just to be sure. Then, finally, he eased away from the building. His legs were shaking, as were his hands, and he was breathing like a bellows. But it looked like he was safe.

For now.

Shaking his head, he started toward where he thought the hill would be—but stopped.

After all, he was already right here. And the office might still be open.

And he'd just burned off a whole bunch of calories. Best to replace them now, while he could.

Chapter Six

Mateo tossed a rock out onto the lake.

It sank like a stone.

"What a bust," he muttered, shaking his head.

Vi hip-checked him to the side, then threw a rock of their own, using a sideways flick of their wrist. The stone hit the dark water at an angle, skipped off its surface, and proceeded to hit and skip six more times before finally exhausting its momentum and disappearing with a faint splash.

"Showoff," Mateo accused, but he was laughing as he said it. "Fine, I suck at skipping stones. It always looks so easy in the movies! But I had hoped to see this Beast."

"Woulda been cool," Nia agreed, shivering a little and wrapping her arms around her lithe form. "And speaking of cool, it's colder down here than up on the hill! Where we left a very nice, very warm little fire. Not to mention all the makings of s'mores."

"Works for me," Vi agreed, sparing the glossy waters one last glance before turning and leading the way back toward their campsite. A few others were still milling about near the water, including one who'd begun strumming a guitar, and though the thrill of possibly seeing the mythic creature had faded, there was still an air of celebration about the shore. Maybe they'd come back down later.

Right now, though, they were regretting not grabbing their hoodie.

And wondering where the fourth member of their little quartet had gone.

Slipping between two campers, they crossed the first dirt road and entered the larger RV area. Vi wasn't exactly tall, and the towering structures loomed on either side like the walls of some metallic canyon. *At least it isn't spooky quiet,* they thought. Voices were all around as people filtered back to their own sites from all along the water's edge. Vi could make out talking, whispering, laughing, even some singing—

—and, somewhere amid all that, they heard another sound.

Hissing.

"Stop!" they ordered, freezing in place. Mateo and Nia did the same. "Hear that?"

After a second, their two friends nodded. "So it decided to take a little midnight stroll?" Nia said. "Get some fresh air?"

"Escape all the tourists gawking at the lake, hoping to take selfies with it," Mateo added. "Can't say I blame it." His grin was visible even in the near dark. "Let's go find it and say hi."

Nia smirked. "Didn't you just say it wanted to avoid all that?" But she still looked around, tilting her head this way and that. "But okay, Mr. Expert Tracker. Which way did it go?"

He, in turn, looked to Vi. "You're the country kid," he pointed out. "I'm just a city boy."

Vi tried to pretend they weren't pleased with the recognition of their skills. "Fine. Come on." And they spun about—until they were facing the lake once more.

"Um, we just came from there," Nia pointed out as Vi started retracing their steps. "And the sounds are coming from somewhere else."

Vi nodded. "Yep. But it's a turtle, right? It's gonna live in or at least near the water. So if it did come ashore, it'll have left tracks where it did. Find those, follow them—"

"And boom, candids with a critter!" Mateo declared, miming taking a selfie. The other two laughed. But Vi was still moving, and their two friends didn't hesitate to follow.

Back by the lake, the guitarist was leading an impromptu singalong. Vi did their best to ignore that for the moment, though, focusing on the banks of the lake. They walked along it, following the edge, concentrating on the strip of land as they went—

They were halfway to the gazebo when they spotted marks in the mud and dirt.

"There." Their two friends gathered with them by the spot, and all three of them stared at the marks there—a wavy line with rounded scoops evenly spaced on either side. "That's from its tail," Vi explained, pointing at the line. "And those are from its webbed feet." They grinned. "Follow that and we find our Beast."

"Sweet!" Mateo clearly wanted to rush along the trail, but restrained himself, bowing extravagantly instead and gesturing for Vi and Nia to go first.

They followed the tracks in among the trailers and campers. But then they hit a patch of drier ground, and the marks simply disappeared.

Vi crouched down, studying the earth there. "I don't get it," they said. "Tracks don't just stop like that. And even on dry land, something that big'd still leave a hefty impression." They frowned. "There's something not quite right about these marks, anyway."

They were still pondering when Nia tapped them on the shoulder. When Vi looked up, their friend gestured for quiet and pointed to the right.

And, now that they had, Vi heard the hissing again. This time they could even make out some clicks mixed in.

Mateo had already noticed or been alerted. He nodded and led the way between two motor homes. With his dark hair and dark shirt, it was difficult to see him, but every so often he'd glance back, grinning, his bright smile like a floating beacon in the dark. Vi kept close behind, and Nia brought up the rear, one long-fingered hand resting on Vi's shoulder.

Reaching the front of those two homes, Mateo glanced around the corner. "There!" he whispered, and the other two crowded close, all three of them peering out.

Perhaps forty feet away, partially hidden behind another RV, was an enormous figure with a massive, scaled head and a barely visible domed body stretching out behind it.

They'd found the Beast of Busco!

For a moment, none of them moved. Then something snapped somewhere nearby, most likely a small branch. The Beast started, twisting this way and that to stare into the night.

Then it slipped back behind the RV and was gone.

"Did you see that?" Mateo asked his friends. Both of them nodded. But while Nia's eyes were wide and bright, Vi's were narrowed behind their glasses.

"You ever see a turtle turn?" they asked. The other two shook their heads. "It has to basically back up, angle forward, back up again, rinse and repeat. Like a tiny little claw-footed car with no reverse gear." They gestured toward where the creature had been. "They sure as hell don't do that!"

Nia smiled. "But this isn't any old turtle, right? It's the freaking Beast of Busco! So maybe it's a little lighter on its feet than you expected, so what? It's still crazy cool we got to see it!"

Suddenly Vi darted forward, cutting across the little clearing to where the Beast had stood. Sharing a glance and a smile, their friends hurried to catch them. By the time they got there, Vi was already down on one knee, studying the ground there.

"Look," they said. "No tracks."

Mateo shrugged. "So? It didn't leave any tracks back there, either. Like Nia said, it's light on its feet."

"And can retract its tail on command?" Vi demanded. "That's not how snapping turtles work." They stood, dusting off their hands and their pants. "It doesn't look right, it doesn't move right—it doesn't even smell right. Something funny's going on."

Just then they heard a shriek, but an identifiably human one. "I just saw it!" someone shouted from what might have been a few rows over. There were answering shouts and yells and whistles, and then the sound of rushing feet as people converged on the area.

"If it wanted anonymity, it's going to be sadly mistaken," Nia pointed out. "But I'd rather not get trampled, and it's still cold out, so what say we get back to our tent and our fire and those s'mores?"

For a moment, Vi didn't budge. Then they sighed. "Fine. Let's hope Andy's back, too." Otherwise they'd have to go looking for him.

Mateo shook his head. "I'm hoping he's not," he admitted. "Otherwise there won't be any s'mores fixings left!"

That was true enough, and the mere thought was enough to spur all three of them to pick up their pace.

CHAPTER SEVEN

Andy found their campsite again more or less by accident, just from stumbling up the hill. That was fine, though, because it looked like his three friends hadn't been back long themselves. Vi was busy stoking the fire, while Nia warmed her hands over the slowly rising flames and Mateo gathered graham crackers, marshmallows, and Hershey bars.

"Hey, just in time for s'mores!" Andy declared as he approached, rubbing his hands together. "Nice!"

"And where have you been, exactly?" Nia asked in that slow drawl she used when she was annoyed or trying to be annoying. Or both.

"Me?" Andy sauntered over and flopped down on the ground by the fire, stretching his full length on his side, one hand on his hip like he was modeling his current ensemble of grubby T-shirt and jeans. "Oh, you know, just the usual—making some new friends, having some good food, getting chased by a huge monster."

That got the desired effect, as the other three all gave him their full attention. Well, Vi was still keeping one eye on the fire. "You saw it?" Mateo asked. "So did we."

"Saw it?" Andy wasn't about to let Mateo steal his thunder. Not this time. "I didn't just see it, I almost ran into it—and then it kept trying to run into, or over, me! Repeatedly!" He described his fearsome encounter in full detail, ending with, "I finally managed to lose it, though. So, y'know, go me."

Vi had finished their campfire duties and was now eyeing Andy. Finally, they shook their head. "No. Just no."

"Whaddya mean, no?" Andy put on his best pout, blinking up at his friend and batting his eyelashes. "You don't believe me?"

They scowled, though he didn't think the expression was really aimed at him. "It isn't you I don't believe," they confirmed after a second. "It's the Beast. I don't think it's real."

Andy sat up. "Um, it's definitely real," he insisted. "I should know, it almost ate me!"

Nia was nodding, and even Mateo looked convinced. But Vi stood their ground.

"Look, you've probably never even seen a turtle except maybe at the zoo, right? Or in the window of a pet store? I have, though. Tons of them in the wild, a dozen different kinds. And I'm telling you, this thing doesn't move like a turtle at all. You said it darted around a corner after you. How? Snapping turtles are faster than most other turtles, sure, but not *that* fast! Or that agile. And especially not if they were that big. When we saw it, same thing. It backed away and disappeared. How?" They shook their head. "I think somebody's messing with people here. It's all a fake."

"Oh." Mollified now that he knew Vi didn't think he was lying—because fibbing or stretching the truth to make it more exciting was one thing, outright falsehood totally another—Andy considered that. "I mean, that mouth looked pretty real, and those eyes. But I wouldn't have thought a turtle could move like that, no."

Nia then told him about their own, slightly more distant and definitely less terrifying encounter, concluding with, "You're right, Vi, I wouldn't know a turtle from a tarantula except by the number of legs, but it didn't move like the ones I have seen. In pet stores and zoos."

Mateo crouched down between Andy and Vi, Nia stepping closer and dropping into a smooth cross-legged stance to complete their little circle. "Okay," Mateo said, not smiling for a change. "Let's say you're right. The Beast isn't real, somebody's just making it look like it is. But something chased Andy. And something backed away from us. That's not just us seeing things, or mistaking shadows. That's, what, a giant puppet? A crazy robot? Some old guy in a rubber fright mask?"

"Whichever it is, you're right, it's deliberate," Nia agreed. "Somebody's behind this whole little charade. So who? And why? Why pretend to be a legendary giant turtle?"

"Drum up business for the town, especially during Turtle Days?" Andy suggested. "That place was packed today! And the guy at the desk here, didn't he say it was way busier'n usual?" He shrugged. "If your town's biggest event is based on this Beast, what better way to get everybody excited than to have the Beast itself show up?"

"And if you can't get the real deal, fake it?" Nia considered, then nodded. "Yeah, that tracks."

"Maybe," Mateo said. "But if that's the case, why not have it sighted downtown or at least along the park, near all the festivities? Why have it show itself all the way out here? It's not like it was holding a sign saying, 'Come see me at the fairgrounds!'"

Just then Andy's stomach growled, as if in reply. His friends all laughed, the tension shattered for the moment. "All right, all right!" Mateo replied, handing out paper plates and then s'more fixings. "I'm working on it!"

"We know who the real beast is around here," Nia joked, nudging Andy. "At least as far as eating is concerned."

"Guilty as charged," Andy admitted. He let himself be distracted by food, like usual. But deep down, he had to admit he was a little disappointed, maybe even a bit hurt. He'd thought he was about to be this famous figure, the handsome young actor/physical comic who'd sighted the legendary Beast of Busco up close and personal and lived to tell the tale. Now that was all ruined—if he did tell anyone, he'd be a laughingstock instead, the guy who let himself get scared by some kid in a costume or something. Best to stay quiet and see what happened next.

Because one thing he was sure of:

Whoever was behind all this had a plan. And they were just getting started.

Chapter Eight

The next day, waiting in line at the bath house, Oscar was all anyone could talk about.

As they approached, the quartet spotted Rob and Jeannie. They greeted and joined the couple, who were grumbling, though good-naturedly.

"Never had to wait for a shower here before," Rob informed them, shaking his head. "The RV section tends to fill up a bit, but of course most of those have their own facilities. Camping area tends to be pretty empty. Not this year, though."

Jeannie nudged him with her shoulder. "It's our own fault," she pointed out, laughing. "If only we'd kept our mouths shut, huh?"

The older couple in front of them turned to join the conversation. "Yeah, you're not wrong," the guy, who was short and grizzled with a neat silvered beard, said. "We usually camp over at Tippecanoe instead. Even bigger lake, and a whole lot prettier — deep, too."

"Deepest natural lake in the region," his partner, whose long hair was a beautiful, snowy white, agreed. "Glacial. It's an extra half hour to here, but worth it." She smiled. "Not this year, though. Not with a chance to finally see the Beast for ourselves!"

"That and the mosquitos," the man added. "Damn things were buzzing all night long, louder'n you can imagine. Couldn't sleep a wink." He shook his head, then shrugged. "So we figured we'd switch over to here instead. Quieter, at least. Even with a giant turtle roaming about."

A few others nearby added their agreement. It seemed that, normally, people made a variety of arrangements on where to camp or park or sleep during Turtle Days. But this year it was all about Blue Lake and trying to catch a glimpse of Oscar.

"So maybe Larry's behind it?" Nia suggested, but quietly, once they'd all used the facilities and were heading back to their tent, the warm early-morning sunlight drying their hair. "He's clearly the one benefiting from these sightings."

Mateo frowned. "I guess. I mean, he's making, what, thirty a night per tent? Figure there's maybe twenty, thirty tents, that's six hundred to almost a thousand a night. And the festival's four days long. People've done stupider things for less."

He didn't sound entirely convinced, though, and privately Vi agreed. For one thing, the campground owner hadn't seemed all that clever. For another, he'd seemed a bit too nice to mess with people like that—maybe distant sightings, but the way he'd spooked Andy hadn't been cool. But there was another big question here.

"Why now?" they asked as they gathered most of their gear and lugged it all back to the van—they'd agreed that it was safer to take everything except the tent with them and set it all back up each night, instead of leaving it here while they were gone. "I'm guessing he's run this place for years, but this is the first time anyone's seen the Beast here. What makes this year any different?"

The others nodded. "Good question," Mateo agreed, holding the driver's door open for Vi—it was their turn to drive today. "What say we poke around at the fair a bit and see if we can come up with any answers?" He winked at them. "First one to solve this thing wins?"

That made Vi grin as they snatched the keys from him. "You're on!"

The park was packed again, and the four friends took a moment after they'd parked to discuss battle plans. "I think I'm gonna ask around, look for that woman we met yesterday, see who else's in charge," Mateo stated. "Maybe they'll know something."

"The marshal, she looked sharp," Nia said. "I'll see if I can find her, get anything out of her."

Andy tapped his chin. "Games and races," he declared after a second. "People talk while they're playing stuff, maybe somebody'll let something slip."

Vi smirked. "Crafts for me. I've got a theory I wanna test." They checked their smartwatch. "Meet at the BBQ tent at one to compare notes?"

Andy's eyes lit up. "Hell, yeah!"

And with that, the four of them split up, each pursuing their own chosen course of action.

Mateo found the organizers easily enough—there was a tent labeled such, right in the center of things. A long table had been set up beneath it, and four people currently sat behind that, ready to greet visitors and answer any questions. One of them was the woman they'd bumped into the day before, Angie Wick.

"Well, howdy again!" she called as he approached. "Guess you decided to stick around, huh? Y'all enjoying yourself?" She had a different Beast of Busco shirt on today, but the same warm smile.

"We did, yes," he answered. "We had such a great time yesterday, we decided to stay for the full festival. Even caught a glimpse of Oscar himself last night, out at Blue Lake."

The man at one end *harrumph*ed. "Back in my day, we didn't need to see him to know he was real," he complained. He was a little older than the other three, with a long, lined face and thinning hair.

"Don't mind Graham," Angie assured Mateo with a friendly wink. "He used to be town mayor and still pines for the good old days. Don't even get me started about his old Army tales. I'm just glad y'all are enjoying yourselves."

"That is great to hear," the other woman there agreed. She was shorter and slimmer than Angie, with sleek dark hair and a more reserved manner but bright eyes. "Samantha Tinsdale," she offered, extending a slender, well-manicured hand. "Turtle Days President."

"Mateo Diaz," he replied, shaking. "This place is impressive. How many of you does it take to run it all?"

"Oh, quite a few," she answered. "Besides myself, Angie, John who's our secretary"—she pointed at the fourth person, a portly, cheerful-looking man with dark curls and beard, who smiled and waved—"and Dennis who's our treasurer, we've got eight board members like Graham here. Then, during the actual event, we've got a whole group of volunteers to run each of the tents, manage the games, sell the food, and so on." She allowed herself a small smile. "We like to say we spend eleven months a year planning, a week running around like crazy, and then three weeks recuperating before we start it up all over again."

"Wow." Mateo didn't have to feign awe and respect. "That's a ton of work. I guess this year's probably busier than ever, too, what with those sightings."

But Samantha shook her head. "Actually, not really. If he'd been seen a month ago, sure, but the first sighting was just the other day. Everybody who was coming had already made their plans." This time, her smile was a bit wider. "Next year, though? Who knows!"

He nodded. "Cool. Well, I'll definitely be telling all my friends about it. Thanks!" He smiled and turned away, heading back out of the tent.

They'd certainly given him some things to think about—and to tell the others.

It didn't take Nia long to locate the marshal—it helped that the woman was tall, and as dark as she was. "Morning," Nia said as she approached, and the woman and the man beside her, a little shorter and wider and a whole lot lighter-skinned but in a matching uniform, turned her way.

"Morning," Rhonda replied. "It was Nia, right? This is Scott Hardenbrook, one of my officers."

He nodded hello. "In for the festival?"

"Actually, we were just passing and saw the posters," she answered truthfully. "But now, absolutely." She glanced around at the chaos. "I'm guessing your people have their hands full, huh?"

The marshal shrugged, though her eyes never stopped scanning the crowds. "Actually, not so much. Most of the folks here are returnees, and of course you've got the locals. They all know each other, at least on sight, so even though there's a lot going on, it tends to be pretty tame. Worst we get is somebody having a little too much to drink and getting in a shouting match with someone who cut in line or beat them at a foot race, stuff like that. We had a pickpocket causing trouble once, a few years back." Her smile was sharp as a knife. "That hasn't happened since."

Beside her, Scott chuckled. "Nope, pretty sure word got out after that one—'don't try that crap around Marshal Cohn!'"

Nia nodded, utterly unsurprised. "I can appreciate that," she said. "I'm from Chicago, and there's neighborhoods like that there, too, where you just know messing around's more trouble than it's worth."

"Chicago?" Those sharp eyes turned toward her for a second. "Yeah, I can hear it. But your one friend, the eater, he sounded East Coast to me. And the other, West Coast? Quite the mix."

"We are," Nia agreed. "And yep, you nailed it, good ear—Andy's from Jersey, Mateo's from LA, and Vi's from Minnesota. We all did a drama program together this past semester, in New York." She shrugged. "We bonded. Andy's uncle has a car dealership, sold a custom job to a guy out in LA and needed someone to drive it there, so we figured we'd do a road trip, stop off at my folks' and Vi's, then see Mateo home, too."

This time the look the marshal gave her was thoughtful—and vaguely approving. "Important to have real friends," she said with what sounded like a wistful note. "And good for you all, seeing the country, trying different things. That's smart."

"Thanks." Nia found herself smiling at the compliment. She had the feeling Rhonda Cohn didn't deliver too many of those. "Well, I won't keep you from your job. Just wanted to say hi. Hope we'll see you again, though." She was a little surprised to realize she meant it.

That earned her another quick smile, a little less reserved than the previous ones. "I'm sure you will. Have fun."

It was both a blessing and a dismissal, and Nia nodded, waved good-bye to Scott, and stepped back into the crowd. She wasn't sure how much she'd learned from that encounter, to be honest. But she did feel like she'd won them an ally if they needed one. And that couldn't help but be a good thing.

Andy was having himself a blast. He'd already come in second in a foot race and first in the hurdles, using his long limbs and boneless agility to advantage. Now he was doing an obstacle course, which was making him work up a serious sweat.

The other contestants so far had been a real mix, ranging from kids to seniors, jocks to nerds, locals to out-of-towners and even a few from other countries. Everybody was friendly, though, even if a few of the jocks did get competitive once the actual events started.

He hadn't learned anything new so far, though. Not really. Almost everybody else here had been before, most of them more than once, and so there was an easy camaraderie about them, like friends who only saw each other once a year but were always happy to reconnect. They'd all welcomed him right away, too, and were already joking about him being the guy to beat at next year's Turtle Days. Most of them were either local or staying here in town, but the few who were out at Blue Lake had caught sight of Oscar as well, and were eagerly sharing those stories with the others, who were just as excited about it.

"I knew it!" one woman about Andy's age exclaimed. She punched the big, beefy guy next to her in the arm, and not lightly. "I told you!"

"Yeah, yeah," he said, wincing a little. "Still just stories. No offense." That last was to the girl who'd just admitted to seeing the Beast by the water, who shrugged.

"You a believer, then?" Andy asked the woman, who had long, straight reddish-blonde hair pulled back in a serviceable ponytail.

She nodded. "Runs in the family." She offered her hand. "Peggy Harmon. My grandfather was Gale Harris. It was his farm where they saw Oscar in 1948 and 1949."

"And she's been trying to prove him right ever since," the guy she'd hit added. He shook with Andy as well, adding, "Tony LaGrange. We're engaged."

"Congrats," Andy said, because he knew that was the sort of thing people said for stuff like that. "Wow, that's ages ago, though. And nobody'd seen it since—until now?"

Peggy sighed. "Yep. My granddad basically ruined himself trying to prove it was real, had to sell the farm and everything. 'Course, the first time anyone saw Oscar was fifty years earlier, so it's not that crazy to think it'd be another seventy, eighty years before he popped up again. Did you know alligator snapping turtles can live into their hundreds? And that they get bigger every year of their lives? So if Oscar's approaching two hundred, stands to reason he'd be huge!"

Tony put an arm around her. "You know I'd love to see you be right," he told her gently. "I would. It's just..." He shrugged. "Biggest one they know of was, what, three hundred pounds? And the size of a big kid? That's nowhere near what the stories claimed, even back then."

Peggy sighed, leaning into him. "I know. I keep hoping, though." She brightened a little. "And now, these new sightings, they sound even bigger!"

Andy decided not to share his own encounter, given their doubts about its authenticity. Instead he just said, "Hey, I hope you get your proof." Fortunately, the judges called for all contestants to line up, and then there wasn't time or breath to talk further.

Still, it was interesting to know there was such a divide in opinion about Oscar. And that some people were desperate for it all to be true. Desperate enough to fake it? That they'd still have to find out.

The man standing in front of the table was as tall as Andy, Vi judged, and more than a bit bulkier, with a long face to match and fine light brown hair. "Hi," he greeted everyone. "Most of you already know me but I'm Craig Rogers. I teach science at CJSHS and I'm a Turtle Days board member." He smiled. "Now, who's ready to make their very own Beast of Busco?"

Everyone there cheered — most of them were a good deal younger than Vi, all the way down to what they guessed were a trio of first- or second-graders, though there were a few older folks and two who might also be college-aged. Vi found themselves sharing a small table with the last two, an older Asian woman, and a small child, and smiled at all of them.

"Hi," they said. "I'm Vi. I use they-them pronouns. First-timer here."

The others all laughed and smiled back. "Welcome, Vi!" the older woman replied. "I'm Fiona, Fiona Chen. I'm on the board with Craig." She indicated the little girl beside her. "And this darling is my granddaughter, Tracy." Tracy's shy smile revealed a missing front tooth.

"I'm Annie," one of the two others introduced herself. "This is Dee."

Dee's smile was as shy as Tracy's, though also excited, and Vi could guess why. Sure enough, they offered, "I'm they-them, too." Their expression brightened when Vi offered a fist bump, which they happily returned.

Then Craig reached their table. "Right," he said, nodding to each of them in turn. "Good to see y'all. Got a newcomer, hey? Welcome!" He had a large plastic container tucked under one arm and reached into that to distribute craft supplies. "So we've got bodies, heads, tails, and legs," he explained as he set out pieces, using his long arm to place them in the table's center. "More than enough to go around, so feel free to make yours a spider-turtle or whatever you like. The limbs all have spaces for joints, or you can just glue them in place for more stability. And for the heads we've got one-piece ones or, if you're feeling more adventurous, I've got some with separate jaws that you can hinge so they really open and close."

Vi had picked up a leg and was examining it. "This is really cool," they offered, which it was, right down to the claws, and with a hole at the top if you wanted to hinge it in place. "3-D printing?"

He nodded. "You got it. I love the thing, use it all the time for class materials. Right, Annie and Dee?" Both of them gave him a thumbs-up. So they were his students, and still excited for this. That was nice. "I'll come back around to answer any questions and help with anything. Once everybody's got theirs built, I'll bring out the paints," he promised before moving on to the next table.

Vi had already focused on the turtle pieces. They loved puppetry and were definitely going to make theirs with proper joints. But they were also impressed by the level of detail involved. They'd only played with 3-D printers a little themselves but knew there was almost no limit to what you could make with one.

Including an enormous Beast, if you had the time, the materials, and the expertise.

Yes, Vi thought, holding a leg up to the body they'd selected. Some of the pieces were beginning to fit together quite nicely.

Chapter Nine

Andy found his friends already waiting in line at the BBQ tent. "Boy, have I got stuff to tell you!" he said as he joined them.

"So do we," Mateo replied. Vi and Nia nodded. "But first, let's eat!"

"Don't have to ask me twice!" Andy agreed, making his friends all laugh. Well, whatever. Finding out stuff was hard work!

They paid for two plates this time, then found a table in the corner so they could talk with at least a modicum of privacy. After that, in between chowing down on ribs, brisket, pulled pork, sausage, and all sorts of sides, each of the quartet filled the others in on what they'd found out during the morning.

Once they'd all had a chance to talk, Vi summed things up. "So we have one guy who easily has the know-how and materials to make a fake Beast," they pointed out, ticking points off on their fingers. "Then we've got one woman who would do just about anything to clear the family name by proving the Beast is real. We've got a ton of people excited about the possibility, and at least one guy who seems oddly disgruntled about it. And of course we've got the festival planners thrilled at the publicity this will bring them. That about cover it?"

But Mateo shook his head. "You're forgetting one," he pointed out, polishing off a bite of pulled pork and mopping his plate with a piece of cornbread. "The one who stands to profit most off Oscar being back."

Nia nodded. "Larry."

"Larry."

Vi frowned. "I mean, yeah, I guess. But that comes back to the question from before — why now? Why not before? This thing's been going on for years."

Mateo shrugged. "Maybe he just ran out of money. Maybe he'd never thought of it before. Maybe he didn't see any way to pull it off until now. Who knows? Point is, he's the only one we know for certain is making money off all this. Even if the festival does gangbusters, that money probably just goes back into its funds for next year, right?"

They all toyed with their food and drink as they considered. "It makes sense," Nia said after a moment. "Though that one guy this morning said something about another lake and it being really noisy. Don't know if that means anything."

"Well, it added to his switching to Blue Lake, where he was more likely to see Oscar," Mateo pointed out. "So maybe? Like, make the competition look bad and yourself look good at the same time, two-pronged attack?"

Andy snagged an onion ring. "So let's say you're right," he commented as he munched. "How do we prove it?"

Mateo tapped the table. "Simple. We ask him." He tapped again. "And if that doesn't work, we snoop around and catch him at it anyway."

That, at least, made Vi laugh. "Okay, we'll try it your way for now," they agreed, finishing their mac and cheese and spinning about to stand up. "Possible Beast, here we come. Oh, and speaking of which—" They reached into their bag and pulled out something they set on the table in front of Andy. "For you. You said you preferred them carry-sized."

Andy goggled a second, then picked up the hand-sized turtle, admiring its jointed limbs and painted shell. "Wow. It's awesome, Vi! Thanks!" And he wrapped his free arm around them in a big hug. Vi's smile was bright enough to light up their whole table.

"That's gorgeous," Nia agreed, studying the figure. "No surprise there." Her friend beamed at her in thanks.

Mateo nodded. "Yeah, top-notch, Vi. You could sell something like that for big bucks, if you wanted." He shared a grin with them. "Now what say we see about catching one just a little bit bigger?"

The campground was mostly empty when they reached it, the majority of its current residents still down at the festival. That made things a bit easier, since Larry was the only person in the office when they entered.

"Hey, y'all enjoying Turtle Days?" he asked as they approached. "Seen the Beast yet?"

"We wanted to ask you about that," Mateo asked, leaning on the counter and staring the owner in the eye. "Have you ever seen it yourself?"

Larry looked away first. "Me? Uh, no, not directly. Heard it plenty, though. That hissing, you can't miss it, huh?"

Andy had been browsing the shelves and now brought a package of hot dogs and another of buns to the counter. "So you told us it was back, but that's only what you heard, huh?" he asked. "Looks can be deceiving though, right?"

The campground owner tugged at his shirt collar, his face a bit flushed. "I mean, yeah, I guess? But sometimes you just gotta have a little faith, ya know?"

"Faith? Not sure what that has to do with anything," Nia countered. "I prefer cold, hard truth, myself. Even if it's not the truth I wanted."

Vi nodded. "Yeah, it's too easy to let yourself get convinced of something by other people. People with their own agendas. Don't you think?"

Larry started. "Huh? Oh, I mean, sure. Gotta make up your own mind and all a' that." He fidgeted with the edge of the hot dog package. "Still, some things're just good no matter what, right?"

The foursome all studied him. He was clearly uncomfortable, but why? They waited, but he didn't add anything further.

Finally, Mateo nodded, pulling out a ten and slapping it onto the counter. "Be seeing you," he warned as he took the food and led the way out of the store. They left Larry staring after them.

"So?" Mateo asked as soon as they were back outside. "He's totally guilty, right?"

Vi scowled. "He's up to something, definitely. Not sure if it's this whole Beast business, though."

"Maybe he just really needed to pee," Andy offered. He shrugged when the others stared at him. "What? It happens!"

"We need to get proof that he's behind the fake Beast," Nia pointed out. "Otherwise, we're still just guessing."

Andy brightened. "We could break into his place, search it for clues."

"Or," Vi said, nudging him, "we could just wait until he closes up and follow him. A lot less illegal that way."

"Oh." Their tall friend bowed his head. "Yeah, I guess that'd work, too." He eyed the food in Mateo's hands. "There's a grill right over there," he pointed out after a second. "Might as well eat while we wait."

The others laughed, but followed him as he headed toward the picnic area. After all, who could say no to a fresh hot dog—or, in Vi's case, a nice, toasted cheese bun?

It was several hours later. The rest of the campers had returned, making the place crowded and noisy for a while. Something had made loud hissing noises just after sunset, prompting a rush toward the lake, but the foursome had stayed put. Perhaps twenty minutes later, most of the other residents started trickling back toward their campers, RVs, and tents, calling it a night.

With almost everyone else in for the evening, the campground was considerably darker, quieter, and colder. Vi shivered as they waited.

"How long are we gonna give it?" Nia asked quietly. "What if he's holed up in there all night? I don't wanna freeze for this!"

She stopped talking, however, when they all heard the creak of a door. Quickly ducking down, the four of them watched as the office opened and Larry emerged. The campground owner glanced this way and that but apparently didn't see them in the dark. Closing the door behind him, they heard him lock it. Then he headed for the parking lot at a rapid clip.

"Don't lose him!" Andy whispered as the owner carefully stepped past the entrance gate.

"How're we gonna lose the only other person walking around?" Nia demanded. Nonetheless, they all quickened their pace, following Larry from a safe distance.

They were still by the gate when he climbed into a red pickup and started it up.

"Crap! Hurry!" Vi urged. The second the pickup had pulled out of the lot, they sprinted for the Sienna, all piling in as fast as they could. Vi had the minivan moving almost before Andy'd pulled the rear door shut.

"There he goes!" Nia said, pointing at a set of receding taillights up ahead. "After him!"

"I know, I know," Vi groused. But they slowed as the pickup approached the main road and turned left onto it. "Huh. He's not heading toward town."

"Maybe he's just going home for the night?" Andy offered from the back seat. "I mean, I would. He probably has better food there." He rubbed his belly and made a face. "Even for me, those hot dogs were a bit suss."

No one commented on the inferior food as they followed Larry down the road a ways. But Vi was smart enough to hang back and not crowd their quarry. That proved useful when the pickup braked and swung onto a side road.

They turned there as well, hanging back even further now that there was no other traffic. "Lights up ahead," Nia declared, studying the scene before them.

Vi got as close as they dared, then pulled over. "Best not to spook him," they pointed out, shutting off the engine.

The others nodded. Together, they all stepped out. The air was cool but not as cold away from the water, and the land was flat enough that they could easily see the pickup ahead of them. It had stopped—right in front of what their eyes gradually adjusted enough to reveal was a large paneled truck.

"Weird place to make a delivery," Mateo whispered, crouching down and sidling closer for a better look. The others followed. They were able to get within a dozen feet, stopping just beyond the arc of the truck's lights.

Larry was there, talking to another man, one with dark hair under a bright blue cap. They chatted a few minutes, and either shook hands or exchanged something small. Then together they walked to the back of the bigger truck, tugging the rear doors open.

Both men disappeared inside for a moment, re-emerging with their arms full of something they carried over to Larry's truck. "Is that… food?" Andy asked in a hushed tone.

Nia snorted. "You think everything's food!" Still, he wasn't wrong. As the light caught one of the objects Larry carried, they could make out the front of a cereal box. "So, what, he's just doing a little late-night shopping?"

"Not from any store, he's not," Mateo corrected. "I think now we know why he was acting so fishy earlier—and why those hot dogs tasted a bit off."

Vi shook their head. "Makes me doubly glad I'm a vegetarian." But they patted Andy sympathetically on the back. "Sorry, dude."

He nodded. "Can we get going, then? I don't think the Beast's showing up all the way out here, do you?"

They made their way back to the Sienna and Vi carefully, quietly eased it down the road and then back to the campground. Then they simply switched it off and sat in the darkened vehicle for a few minutes.

Sure enough, the red pickup pulled in shortly after that. They waited until its owner was out and fishing in the truck bed before emerging and converging on him.

"Hey, Larry!" Andy said, walking over to slap the startled man on the back. "Whatcha got there? Cheerios?" He snatched the big yellow cereal box from Larry's hands. "Huh, looks like these're expired, though, huh? Probably shouldn't sell 'em, then, right? Wouldn't want people ta get sick or anything."

"What?" The campground owner stared at each of them. "I… uh, no. No, of course not."

Nia was sorting through the stuff in the truck bed, using the flashlight on her phone. "Hey, these're expired too, Larry. And these. And these."

"It's all expired, isn't it?" Mateo asked, hands on his hips. "You buy expired food on the sly, then sell it in your store at full price. That's pretty low."

Larry wiped sweat from his forehead. "I'm not doing anything illegal!" he sputtered. "It's all still good!"

"You sure about that?" Vi asked. "Think the FDA'd agree? Should we give them a call and find out?"

The man sagged against his truck. "What do you want?" he asked, his voice as deflated as the rest of him. "Your money back?"

"We want to know about the Beast," Mateo replied. "Are you behind that?"

Larry stared at him. "What?"

"Did you fake these new sightings to drum up business?" Nia demanded, her voice sharp and no-nonsense.

"No!" The campground owner flailed his hands. "I don't know anything about that! I'm just happy it showed up when it did! I'm making out like a bandit!"

The foursome all stared at him, but after a moment Vi sighed and turned away. "He's not lying," they decided.

The others gave it another second, but Larry looked almost in tears and finally they relented. "Stop with the past-due food, dude," Mateo warned. Andy nodded but kept the box of Cheerios as they walked away.

"Okay, that was a bust," Mateo said as they trekked back toward their campsite. "Now what?"

Nia and Andy shook their heads—but Vi grinned. "Now," they declared, "we do one of my favorite things." They laughed, even as their friends groaned in response to their next word:

"Research!"

Chapter Ten

It was Andy's turn behind the wheel, and he maneuvered the Sienna with the casual carelessness of an urban driver using a vehicle he didn't own. Sitting directly behind him, Vi kicked his seat more than once. "We *are* getting paid to deliver it intact," they reminded him sharply after he narrowly missed taking out a mailbox on a wide turn.

"Relax," Andy answered, not bothering to look over his shoulder — or to set his other hand on the wheel. "I got this." He glanced over at Nia, who had her phone out. "Where're we going again?"

Mateo snorted from the other back seat. "You can't possibly get lost," he chided. "This town's got all of five streets!"

Andy pulled himself up in his seat. "I am not lost," he declared loftily. "I am exploring my surroundings." He batted his eyes at Nia. "So, where are we going?"

She made a vague puking gesture but fed him directions anyway, and soon they had passed the turnoff for the fairgrounds and were continuing on down Main Street, with shops and stores on either side. And churches. "Why would a town this size need more than one?" Andy asked, but even he knew better. Besides which, it was actually nice that people here had a choice.

Just ahead of the second church they could see a familiar Y-intersection, complete with two statues. But on the block before that stood an old red brick building with white trim, and Andy pulled up alongside it. The clean white lettering on the big plate glass window in front read, "Churubusco History Center."

"Not sure how much history a town this size can have," Nia muttered as they all exited the vehicle, earning her a swat on the shoulder from Vi. "Yeah, fine, whatever."

Vi led the way into the building — fortunately, the door proclaimed that their operating hours were ten am to two pm and it had just passed the former. A bell tinkled as they pushed the door open, and an older man appeared from the back, wearing a warm smile.

"Welcome!" he proclaimed as Mateo shut the door behind him. "I'm Davey Gilmore, director of the Churubusco History Center. Is it your first time here?" He nodded. "I don't recognize y'all, and we ain't that big a place, so I'm guessing you're not local. Here for Turtle Days?"

"Not originally," Vi answered truthfully. "But we saw the signs and couldn't resist. And now we figured we'd learn more about the town in general."

Davey laughed. "Well, you came to the right place for that! My buddy Dave Armistad and I — yes, two Daves, no waiting — opened this place sixty years ago now and you won't find a bigger collection of information, images, and items about our little slice of Heaven!" He led them back behind the front counter and into a small warren of narrow corridors between tall display cases, keeping up a running patter the entire time. Vi was fascinated and stayed close by, peppering the old man with questions, but the other three hung back a bit.

"So these are all pictures of this town?" Nia said, studying an image labeled "1907 Busco." "Gotta admit, that's kinda cool."

"I guess," Andy said, tapping a knuckle against the glass. "If you like things in black and white. Or brown and white? Gray?"

"It's history, bonehead," Mateo told him. "And Nia's right, it's kind of cool. Didn't you ever look at pictures of New York back in the day to see what it was like then?"

Andy shrugged. "Why should I? I wasn't there to enjoy it."

The other two sighed and gave up, quickening their steps to catch up with Vi and Davey. Fortunately, they'd stopped by another case, this one showing a large lantern.

"This is the very light used to search for Oscar in 1949," the director was explaining. "That was back when Gale Harris had seen the Beast on his farm, but nobody would believe him. Poor fella, he spent years — and every cent he had — trying to prove it."

That did interest Andy, at least. "Yeah, I met his granddaughter," he offered. "She seemed like a believer, herself."

Davey nodded. "Peggy, sure. Good kid. Loved her granddad something fierce. Used to stick up for him whenever people'd snicker about it." He sighed. "Not that it did Gale any good, in the end."

"But that wasn't the first sighting, right?" Mateo asked. "We heard there was an even earlier one."

"There was," Davey agreed. "Back in 1898, by Oscar Fulk. That's who our Oscar is named after. Only, he didn't have any proof, either, and it was just his word. Then, in July of 1948, a whole fifty years later, two locals were out fishing and claimed they saw the Beast themselves. That was on Gale's property, up by Madden Road, and he said he saw it, too. While mending his roof, with the town pastor beside him, no less. And this time, word got out." He smiled. "For a little while, we were famous. Folks came from all around, hoping to see Oscar. They brought in deep-sea divers, they tried damming the lake — which Gale named 'Fulk Lake' in the original Oscar's honor — they tried all kinds of things. But nobody saw him, or at least not that they could prove. And eventually Gale ran out of money and had to sell the farm."

Nia frowned. "But they still started a festival about him. The Beast, I mean. Even though nobody's sure he's even real."

"They did," Davey told her. "Same way there are Bigfoot festivals and Yeti ones and so on." He smiled. "People love a bit of mystery, and they especially love having something nobody else does. A monster that's only found here, and only seen by a few people over the last hundred years? Oscar's the biggest thing to ever happen to Churubusco. Of course we were gonna celebrate him!"

They explored the rest of the history center, admiring many of the old photos and some of the other town artifacts, but didn't find anything to shed light on recent events. "Thank you so much," Vi told the director as they all headed out. "This was really great." They meant it, too. Vi loved history.

He beamed at her. "You are very welcome, all of you. Come back any time, and tell your friends, too. Oh, and enjoy the rest of Turtle Days!"

"Nice guy," Mateo commented at they made for the car. "But can you imagine working in a place like that, running it, for all those years? Wow."

Vi's smile didn't dim a bit. "It's called dedication," they replied. "And I think it's admirable."

"You would," Andy muttered, then yelped as they punched him in the arm. "Aw, come on, I'm still bruised from the last time!"

Retracing their steps by a few blocks, they returned to the festival. But as they were parking, Mateo spotted someone lurking among the cars. "Hey, who's that over there?" he asked.

The others all followed his gaze. "Dunno, but whoever it is, seems like they don't wanna be seen," Nia answered. She grinned. "Let's go find out why."

The four of them crowded single file into the narrow lane between the cars and the backs of the booths, moving down it as quietly as possible. "Why're you in front of me?" Vi groused at Andy, who towered over them. He just shrugged and grinned back at them with a wink.

They heard sounds up ahead of somebody talking and laughing. More than one, from the noise. Mateo, who was in front, got as close as he dared, stopping behind a big, beat-up old Jeep. Then they all gathered behind the vehicle and peered around or over it.

On the Jeep's other side, in an empty parking space, loitered a trio of teens. Vi recognized them at once.

"It's the three from the Subway," they whispered. Their friends nodded. "Maybe they're the fake Beast, just to mess with people?"

They all stayed quiet a few minutes, watching the kids. But at the moment they were just talking, laughing, and pushing each other. Finally, though, one of them—the same one who'd messed with Vi—said, "I'm bored. Let's bounce."

His two friends nodded and fell into step beside him as he turned and walked away with that slouching gait typical of too-cool teens everywhere.

"Think he's going for an Oscar costume?" Andy asked once the trio were too far away to hear them.

They all frowned, finding it unlikely the teens could be behind anything so complex. Still, they didn't have any better leads, so when Mateo set off after the trio, the others followed.

They soon found themselves approaching the far end of the festival. Up ahead, the three boys had slowed, and then ducked behind the Port-a-Potties set up there. "I am not following them back there," Nia declared.

"Naw, we'll just wait here," Vi agreed. "And see what they've got when they come back out."

Sure enough, the trio soon re-emerged, and it was clear from the way they were hunched and giggling that they had indeed retrieved something from some hiding place. By this time, however, Mateo was tired of waiting.

"Hey!" he called, striding forward. The teens started, staring and flushing exactly like kids caught doing something they shouldn't. "What do you think you're doing?"

The lead boy stammered, then blinked as he finally saw who was accosting him. "You! What the hell do you want?" he sneered. "You're not even from around here!"

"Maybe not," Nia agreed with a sharp smile. "But we *do* know the marshal. Should I go get her?"

That had the boys turning pale. "No!" the one on the right begged. "We're not doing nothing wrong!"

"Yeah, we're just having a little fun," the one on the left agreed. "No big deal." But he was shaking as he made that claim.

"What's in your hands?" Andy demanded, stepping up and grabbing the first kid's arm. The teen jerked away—and several small red spheres fell from his grip to bounce at their feet. He went to grab them, but Andy was quicker, scooping them up with his long reach. "Cherry bombs," he said, holding one of them up to display the long wick. "I'm betting these aren't on the approved list of Turtle Days activities."

"So what?" the lead boy snapped. "It's nothing to you!" But he flinched when Vi stomped up and got in his face.

"Hand them over," they insisted, and after a second he caved and surrendered the firecrackers. His two friends did likewise.

"Now git!" Nia barked, and the boys took off running, almost tripping over their own feet in their haste. They were several car lengths away before their leader turned to give them the finger.

"Well, that was a bust—again," Mateo said as they watched the teens flee. "They're delinquents, sure, but they've got nothing to do with this whole Beast business."

Andy nodded, but he was smiling as he started juggling the cherry bombs he held. "Hey, at least it wasn't a total loss. We've got these now. Could make nights at the campground a whole lot more interesting."

"Don't even think about it," Nia warned, and he laughed. But didn't stop tossing the little firecrackers round and round and round.

Chapter Eleven

"So…" Andy started, finally catching and tucking the cherry bombs away as they retraced their steps toward the festival proper.

Vi giggled and checked their watch. "Is it lunch time already?"

"Well, now that you mention it…" But their lanky friend would not be distracted by the notion of food, for once. "No, about this whole Beast thing. I told you I met that one woman, the farmer's granddaughter, right? Peggy Harmon. What if she's behind it all?"

The others paused by the Sienna, the sounds of the nearby fair washing over them but still distant enough that they could carry on a proper conversation without shouting. "Could be," Nia said. "If it were my gramps, I'd do anything for him, too."

"Same," Vi agreed. "If she is, though, you said her boyfriend didn't know anything about it?"

Andy nodded. "Yeah, fiancé but not a believer, and if he was in on it why's he so public about not thinking it's real? Sounds counterproductive."

"Maybe to throw people off?" Mateo suggested. "You know, have them thinking exactly like you are, that they can't be behind it if he's actively dissing the idea?" He grinned. "One way to find out, right?"

"Question them?" Andy asked. He brightened. "Over food?"

Nia shoved him. "No, you goof. Find them and follow them. If they really are pretending to be the Beast, they've gotta have that gear stashed somewhere."

Vi frowned. "Okay, but there're a lot of people here. What do they look like?" That last was directed at Andy.

He scuffed the ground with the tip of his shoe. "Uh, she was… blonde? I think? Long hair? Wearing, I dunno, jeans and a tee-shirt? And he's big, burly. Real farm-boy type."

"Great," Nia drawled. "A long-haired blonde and a big guy. Here. That's sure to stand out."

Vi was studying Andy. "Would you even recognize them if you saw them again?" It was a fair point—Andy was great with remembering show tunes and movie quotes, and restaurants and menu items. People, not so much.

But this time he nodded confidently. "Yeah, absolutely." He grinned at the rest of them. "So I guess you'll just have to follow my lead."

"Ten bucks says it takes us straight back to the BBQ tent," Mateo muttered to Nia none too quietly, and both she and Vi smothered laughs as Andy looked aggrieved. But none of them had any better ideas, so they traipsed after him as he passed through the parking lot and entered the chaos that was the Turtle Days festival's third day.

It was just as much of a madhouse as it had been the other two days. People were everywhere, talking and laughing and shouting. Little kids were darting through the crowd waving streamers and Turtle Day flags and cotton candy. Older people were moving more slowly, forcing others to flow around them. After a few minutes, when they'd barely moved past the first row of stalls, Nia sighed. "This is hopeless," she stated. "How're we gonna find anyone in all this?"

Vi, who was the shortest of them, nodded—but then smiled. "I've got an idea." They led the others over to the side, where there was a fenced-off area for races and other physical contests. Stands had been set up around the edges, and Vi slipped onto those, heading for the top row. Fortunately, it seemed they were between events, because only a few people were there, taking advantage of a place to sit.

"Nice one, Vi," Mateo said as they all joined them at the top. Facing backward, they could see out over most of the fair. "Okay, Andy, tell us when you see her."

Andy nodded and got to work scanning the crowd. But there were just so many people! And a bunch of them had long blonde hair, or were big! "There!" he said, stabbing a finger at a woman. "Oh, no, never mind," he amended as he got a better look at her face and saw that she was, like, his mom's age. "Over… no, that's not her. Maybe there?" He was getting less sure of himself the more people he saw. It didn't help that they were above the crowd so everyone was a lot smaller and harder to make out.

Nia groaned, resting her arms on the back rail and putting her head down on them. But Vi pitched in. "What about those two?" they said, indicating a pair by the cotton candy. "Or those?" With them directing Andy's attention, he could focus on just those people rather than trying to see everyone at once.

And their combined efforts paid off. "There!" he said, waving at the fourth couple Vi had found. "That's them!"

Mateo eyed the pair, who were by one of the crafts booths. "You sure?" They did fit the description, at least, and seemed about the right age.

"Positive," Andy insisted. Then he sagged. "But they're splitting up!" Sure enough, the guy had turned toward the food area while the woman had started toward the parking lot.

"Follow her," Vi declared, already rising to their feet. "If she's going off-site, it's more likely she'll take us to what we need."

The others agreed and stood as well, all of them making haste down off the bleachers and back to their own car. They had just reached the parking lot when a dark green pickup pulled out. Peggy was clearly visible at the wheel.

"After that car!" Andy shouted, sprinting toward the Sienna. "Oh, yeah, I'm driving!" With a laugh, he yanked the door open and slid behind the wheel, already firing up the engine as the others piled in. "Let's go, team!"

"Don't crowd her," Nia warned as he backed out of the space with a screech of tires. "We don't want to spook her."

Andy waved off the advice. "Yeah, yeah. I've seen at least as many spy shows as you have, I know what I'm doing."

Fortunately, the traffic was light—most of the town was here at the festival already. It was easy enough to spot the green truck as it headed back the way they'd come earlier, past the History Center. When it made a left onto East State Road, they followed, just close enough to see where she was going.

"Well, wherever it is, it's out of town," Mateo remarked as the houses gave way to farmland. "Hope she's not done for the day."

"Seems a bit early for that," Vi offered. "And if she was, wouldn't he have gone with her? Naw, she's on a mission."

They passed a sign for a small local airport. There were only a handful of roads intersecting the one they were on, which was now labeled "Route 205."

"Any ideas?" Andy asked from the driver's seat. "You really think she lives out here?"

"It's farmland," Vi reminded him. "Houses are way far apart, so yeah, she definitely could."

Nia, who had kept her eyes on the pickup, sat up. "She's turning!"

Sure enough, the truck had slowed and was making a left onto a road that ran straight north. "Madden Road," Mateo read as they followed.

Beside him, Vi frowned. "Madden?" Then they smiled. "I know where she's going!"

Andy glanced at her in the rearview. "Okay, care to share with the class? And please, please let it be a restaurant!"

They smirked at him. "No, it's Fulk Lake! Or at least her grandfather's old farm. That was out here off Madden Road!"

Mateo nodded slowly. "What better place to hide a fake Beast than where it was first spotted. Nice one, Vi!"

Their prediction proved true when, a few minutes later, the pickup turned left again, onto Clark Chapman Ditch—"not thrilled about driving on that," Andy groused—and past a "Land For Sale" sign. "Hunting, ranch, farm, timber," it read below that.

"Her grandfather had to sell the place, back in the day," Vi reminded the others. "Guess the current owners are doing the same."

Indeed, up ahead they could see an old farmhouse. Andy slowed to a stop as the pickup pulled up there, and the four friends squinted, trying to see from here. "Looks abandoned," Nia offered, taking in the building's rundown state and lack of lights or any signs of life.

"Not completely," Vi countered as Peggy headed for the front door—which opened before she reached it. A slim, dark-haired figure stepped out—and, as they watched, the two embraced.

"Uh..." Nia said. "That's not her fiancée, right? Because there's nothing platonic about that greeting!"

"Definitely not," Andy agreed. "On both counts."

Vi was still staring as the couple disappeared inside the house. "So maybe that's why he acted so surprised, because he really doesn't know anything about it? It's just those two who're behind it all?"

But Nia shook her head. "I don't think they're pretending to be Oscar in there," she said gently, and Vi blushed. "Looks like just an old-fashioned case of hooking up to me."

"Poor girl probably can't admit her real interests to anyone around here," Mateo agreed, and the others all nodded. For various reasons, that was something they could all understand. "Come on, let's give them their privacy."

Andy restarted the car and slowly backed it away down the road until he could turn onto the rural route. "Sorry, guys," he said after the farm had disappeared in the rearview. "Guess that was a bust."

Mateo patted him on the shoulder. "No worries, man. We've all had swings and misses so far." He smiled. "On the plus side, pretty sure I spotted a pizza place as we were heading out of town. Who's up for a slice?"

Andy's only response was to gun the engine, sending the minivan hurtling forward as the others fell back in their seats, laughing.

Chapter Twelve

After availing themselves of Papa's Place's plentiful pizza, grinders, and impressive salad bar, the foursome discussed what to do next.

"Back to the fair?" Vi suggested. "Maybe we'll see something we missed."

None of the others had any better idea, so they hopped back into the Sienna and drove the handful of blocks up Main Street to the park and the fairgrounds. Turtle Days, Day Three was still just as busy as the previous two, and before they'd even exited the parking lot they could hear the noise of the large, energetic, excited crowd.

"How big is this town, again?" Mateo asked as they stood there on the threshold, staring at the mob ahead of them.

Vi, who had of course looked up details the other night, answered, "Around nineteen hundred."

Mateo squinted at the crowd. "There's got to be, what, two to three thousand here? Maybe as many as four? Feels like the whole town is here, and then some."

The others shrugged. "I'm no good at counting heads," Nia said. "But the rest of the town feels pretty empty, yeah. Though maybe that's just a small-town thing." She said the last while eyeing Vi in case they decided to respond with violence.

But Vi was more interested in Mateo's observation—and the perceived reason behind it. "You're wondering if these Oscar sightings have already bumped up attendance here, just like they did at the campgrounds," they noted. "Could be. They told you it hadn't, right? But they could've been lying, or even just being cautious while the event's still going on. We don't have any idea where all the money goes, really. Though I did check out the Turtle Days social media, and they're all volunteers."

"So the money's probably going back into the organization, to fund next year's event," Mateo said. "That makes sense, and fits with what they told me." He shrugged. "It was worth a thought." He spotted someone in the crowd, a tall older man with a long face. "There's one of the Board now, actually. I think his name was Graham something. He used to be mayor."

Vi was studying the man next to Graham, who was equally tall and had similar features but was a good deal younger. "That's Mr. Rogers," they said, and glared at the others when they laughed. "What, it's his name! He teaches science. He was the one who had us making model Oscars." They frowned, remembering. "I think he said he was a Board member, too."

The others nodded at that, but Mateo was still focused elsewhere. "Why wouldn't they want to bring their fake Beast here, whoever they are?" he asked now. "I mean, if the goal's to get everybody all worked up about the Beast being back, the more people who see it, the better. And what place more perfect for that than the festival held in its honor?"

"Too risky," Nia guessed. "Broad daylight, tons of witnesses, and all it takes is one slip-up — or one person paying too close attention — and the gig is up."

But Andy shook his head. "We don't know enough," he stated, waggling his hands. "Like the really big stuff. I mean, okay, it's probably not real, I get that. It's somebody in a really good costume, most likely 3-D printed like Vi said. But who's under all that get-up? And is it really just a publicity stunt? I think we're missing something. No idea what, though."

Vi grimaced. "You're right," they admitted. "We need to know more. And the best way to do that is to catch this fake Beast and find out who it really is."

"Ooh!" Mateo rubbed his hands together. "We can set a trap for it!"

Nia raised an eyebrow at him. "What, like with a carrot on a string? You don't think it'll notice? It's not a rabbit!"

He just grinned at her. "I know that. And I was thinking something a little bigger than a carrot — and a whole lot more enticing."

He told them what he had in mind. Nia stared at him like he was nuts but Vi seemed to be seriously considering it. Andy, of course, loved the idea.

"Dibs if it doesn't show!" he declared, even though they'd literally just eaten. The others groaned, but they were all watching Vi for the final verdict.

Finally, they nodded. "It could work," they admitted. "And if it doesn't, we didn't lose much. I can't think of anything better, so might as well give it a go."

"Y'all really think this will work?" Nia drawled, standing back as Mateo and Vi arranged things in the clearing between Blue Lake's gazebo and the more overgrown section designated a "Natural area" on the map.

"Why not?" Andy asked from beside her. "I mean, who doesn't like pizza, right?"

Vi actually nodded, even though the one in question had pepperoni and sausage. "It does smell really good," they admitted, sitting back to check their work. "Almost makes me wish I'd done that for lunch, instead of the salad. Though that was really good, too. Anyway, turtles are largely omnivorous, especially snapping turtles. Besides which, something that big would need a lot of fuel, meaning it should be as perpetually hungry as Andy is."

Nia scoffed at the notion. "Not sure that's possible, but okay, let's say you're right. It comes out of the water, smells the pizza, sees it, leans in to take a bite, and then what?"

"To do that, it's got to step in close," Mateo answered. He indicated the rope coils they'd placed in a circle around the open pizza box, and the rope's other end that he held in his hand. "The second it plants one of its feet in that circle, we yank the rope, cinching it tight around the leg and pulling it off the ground. Then we loop the rope around that tree you're standing by, and it's stuck. We unmask whoever it is, question them, and case solved."

"Right, 'cause a person in a turtle costume's still gonna behave like a real giant turtle and just think, 'hey, a free pizza, yummy'?" was Nia's next question.

Vi smiled. "At the very least, they'll probably be curious enough to take a closer look, and that'll work just as well for our purposes."

Andy was eyeing the pizza, which was still steaming slightly. "How much time are we giving this before we call it a bust and I get the pie?" he asked, licking his lips.

"Slow down there, champ," Vi warned. "Worse comes to worst, I'll buy you one of your own, okay?" Their friend nodded, but still hadn't looked away from the food.

Once Vi and Mateo finished patting down leaves to mask the rope, they retreated behind the nearest RV with the others. The sun was just starting to set. "Now we wait," Vi said. "It's only been seen at night—which makes sense if it needs the dark to cover any flaws—so any time now."

They settled in. The temperature began to drop as the light faded, leaving them all shivering a little, and before long they were wishing for the comfort of their campfire, but none of them moved. "If it's not here by midnight, we give up for the night," Mateo whispered at one point, causing Nia and Andy to wince.

"Midnight! I'll be a very well-dressed popsicle long before that!" Nia complained, but quietly. They had all agreed to this, after all.

They heard other campers around, but no one walked through the clearing, which was a relief. Their efforts might have been hard to explain, otherwise!

More time passed. The night grew darker, and colder. They could see their breath, even though it was June. "Not sure how much longer I can stand this," Nia warned softly.

Vi started to reply, saying they didn't all have to stay—they were more used to the cold than their friends—when they heard that same hissing as the other night. "It's coming!" Everyone straightened at once, discomfort forgotten.

A moment later, a big, bulky figure stepped from the shadows. Hook-beaked head, four thick, clawed feet, a long tail, and a domed body in between.

It was the Beast.

"Get ready!" Vi whispered, and Mateo nodded beside her, numbed hands tightening around the rope.

They all watched as the Beast lumbered forward, its body swaying with each step.

It stopped before the pizza—but just beyond the concealed rope traps.

It bent forward slightly, peering down at the food.

It sniffed.

Then, with a sound like a chuckle, it raised one foot to stomp directly on the pie itself.

That was too much for Andy. "Hey!" he shouted, straightening and stepping out from behind the RV. "No messing with good food!"

The Beast swung to face him. For an instant, they glared at each other, the pizza between them.

Then the giant turtle spun about, its tail nearly whipping Andy in the face, and bolted toward the volleyball court.

"Save that pie!" Andy shouted over his shoulder, and took off in pursuit.

With a sigh, Vi, who was the shortest of them, scuttled forward, deftly avoiding the ropes, and scooped up the box, shutting it securely before following the rest of their friends and a panicked giant turtle.

Andy could barely see where he was going, but it didn't matter. He was following the Beast by sound as it crashed into this RV and that camper, careening off each one without losing its momentum. Darn, that thing was fast!

He could hear his friends racing after him, and appreciated the support. But when it came to running, Andy knew he had them all beat. If anybody was going to catch Oscar right now, it was him.

The irony of him chasing the thing, when just the other day it had been the other way round, did not escape him. Fortunately, it also didn't slow him down any.

The ground changed from dirt and grass to sand as they reached the beach. For a second Andy thought the Beast might tangle itself in the volleyball net and save them all a lot of trouble, but it skirted that and charged onto the road past it instead. At this time of night the dirt road was empty — probably everyone was heading for the lake to see if they could spy the Beast again, not realizing it was sprinting in the other direction!

Andy was running full-out, but he wasn't closing the distance at all. How was that possible, he wondered. That thing had to be close to a ton, and it had four legs and a tail!

Up ahead he saw the RVs come to an end, and a marked-off rectangle on the grass beyond, with a single post at each end holding a glass square and a metal hoop. The basketball court. That was opposite the office — and right before the campground's entrance.

If the Beast made it past the gate, Andy suspected he'd never catch it.

He put on a burst of speed, hoping to take it by surprise. But the sight of freedom had apparently spurred the creature as well. It also sped up, shooting across the court.

Then it hurdled the gate—only, its hind legs caught fast, stopping it dead for a second.

"Yes!" Andy breathed. Now was his chance!

The Beast glanced back at him. It shuddered.

Then it tore itself free—by ripping its own body in half!

"Gross!" Andy cried, trying to stop and not run into the grisly body now draped over the gate. But he was going too fast. He slammed into the body and the bar pinning it there, and flipped over it, slamming onto his back on the dirt and gravel beyond. "Oof!"

Meanwhile, what was left of the Beast was stumbling away.

Andy shook himself off, caught his breath, and pushed up into a crouch. His head hurt and his vision swam, but he could just make out the maimed creature staggering across the road and to the vehicles parked in the lot beyond.

Was it… he squinted, trying to make sense of what he saw.

Was it climbing into a small truck?

A minute later, as his friends caught up and helped him to his feet, Andy saw headlights blink on. "Stop that truck!" he cried. But it was too late.

The four of them all stared as a dusty blue pickup backed out of a space and then came barreling out onto the road, racing away in a screech of tires.

"Well," Mateo commented, brushing some dirt off Andy's back as Vi wordlessly handed him the pizza box. "That didn't exactly go as planned."

"No," Nia agreed, having stopped at the gate. "But it does prove one thing." She indicated the Beast's severed body, lifting it up as the others turned back to join her there. "Definitely a fake."

Close up, Andy could see that the "body" was in fact an empty shell, and not the kind a turtle would have. This one was cloth around a framework of thin, curved metal rods. "Hey, it's one of those pop-up tents!"

Vi nodded, inspecting one of the hind legs. "Molded plastic," they confirmed, tapping a claw with their finger. "Three-D printed, has to be. Pretty sure I know who made it—and probably wore it. We can find out tomorrow who owns that truck, but easy money says it's one Craig Rogers, high school chemistry teacher."

"So that's part of the puzzle solved," Mateo said, frowning at the abandoned Beast costume. "We know the who, and at least part of the how. The big question, still, is why."

Andy nodded, half a slice already stuffed in his mouth. "We can ask tomorrow," he offered around the big bite. "Right now, though, know what I really need?" His three friends waited. "Some Coke, to wash this down."

They laughed, but Mateo did take a slice of his own. Andy didn't argue. They'd all earned it.

The next morning, Nia snagged the keys out of Vi's hand when they reached the car. "My turn behind the wheel!" she declared. Vi groaned but couldn't very well argue. They had all agreed before they'd set out that, since all four of them had licenses, they'd take turns.

But Nia was a Chicagoan, which was as bad as a New York driver in Vi's book. She took other vehicles on the road as a personal affront, and any space in the lanes ahead of her as a challenge.

Andy, of course, was completely used to it, since New Jersey drivers were much the same. He just couldn't be bothered to be that aggressive, was all. Mateo's LA style was a little more defensive. Vi, having been raised in a quieter part of the country, was the least comfortable with heavy traffic or high-speed lane changes, but knew better than to complain. And did their best to keep their gasps to themself.

Once they'd reached the fairgrounds—in one piece, with only a few near-misses—Vi led the way toward the craft tent. They were surprised, however, to step into its shade and discover, not the tall, broad form of Craig Rogers but a smaller, sleeker figure with close-cropped dark hair. This one was also familiar to them, though, and broke into a big smile when she saw them. Especially Mateo.

"Hey, y'all!" she called, setting down a plastic container and crossing toward them. "This is a nice surprise!"

Nia, who was good at faces and names, muttered to him, "Cindy from Subway," and Mateo, putting his performing skills to good use, acted like he'd remembered that all along, stepping forward to greet the girl.

"Hi, Cindy!" he replied. "Good to see you, too. I was going to text later, but this is even better."

Vi nodded hello as well, but was busy scanning the otherwise empty tent. "Where's Mr. Rogers?" they asked, and winced when they heard that come out of their mouth.

Cindy just laughed. "Don't worry, he's heard that one a million times," she promised. "He just laughs it off."

"You had him for science," Nia guessed, and the other girl nodded.

"Yeah, junior year—which was already a few years back," she added pointedly, fluttering her eyelashes at Mateo. Andy was polite enough to turn away while he rolled his own eyes at the display. "He's a great teacher, great guy. I've helped him out here a couple times in the past, it's good fun."

"So he's on his way?" Mateo asked, but Cindy shook her head.

"Naw, said he wasn't feeling well today, so I'm covering for him. Though I wouldn't be surprised if that was just an excuse and his uncle's got him running errands or something. Seen that happen more than a few times before. Or maybe he's getting ready for the parade, that starts pretty soon. Hey, wanna help? I sure wouldn't mind the company." She was kind enough to aim that remark at all four of them, though it was obvious who she really meant.

Mateo smiled in response. "Love to, but we've actually got something we need to take care of today. Are you around later, though?"

"Oh, definitely!" she answered. "Last night of the festival, so there's fireworks at dusk—though some people set off their own even earlier. Then they've got parade awards with all the floats lined up again, plus music and giveaways and finally the big laser light show down Main Street, too. I'll be done here by six."

"Perfect," he told her. "Meet you back here then. We can grab a bite, maybe, and check out the fireworks and the rest."

The others all said their goodbyes too, and half-dragged Mateo from the tent. "Come on, Romeo," Nia told him as they exited. "Work now, flirt later."

He nodded, regaining focus once they were clear. "Right. Only problem is, we were counting on questioning him here. Where does that leave us?"

The others had been pondering the same question—and it was Andy who offered an answer. "We were figuring he was doing that whole Beast routine to draw people in, right?" their lanky friend asked. "But what if we've got it backward?"

"He was trying to drive people away?" Vi shook their head. "If that was the case, it backfired big time. But he kept at it anyway. That doesn't make any sense."

Andy wasn't done, though. "No, not driving people away from Blue Lake," he said. "But getting them away from somewhere else, and all paying attention to him there."

Mateo snapped his fingers. "That older couple," he said, "the ones by the bath house. They said they usually camp somewhere else, but it was too noisy this year, and they were curious about Oscar anyway."

"Tippecanoe," Vi confirmed, holding up their phone. "I looked it up after that, and it's just like they said—glacial lake, deepest natural body of water in the area, maybe twenty minutes away." They gave Andy a careful, assessing look. "You think this was all to get people away from there?"

He shrugged, not used to being taken so seriously, but added, "Yeah, could be, right? I mean, if that's the case, it worked. Everybody's either here or at Blue Lake."

"Worth checking out, if nothing else," Mateo agreed. He held out his hand to Nia. "Keys?"

She just laughed at him. "Nuh-uh. But you can navigate." And, with a flourish, she spun and led the way back to the car.

"Well, it's pretty, all right," Vi remarked as they pulled up. "Big, too. Where do we start?"

Andy had been studying an online map as they drove. "What about here?" he asked. "The Edmund & Virginia Bell Nature Preserve. It's basically the far-right corner of Tippecanoe, between that and James Lake."

"Works for me," Nia agreed, spinning the wheel and reversing the Sienna in a quick, tight turn. A minute later they were facing a turn without a sign, only a small, squared stone post containing a mailbox. "This the right place?"

Andy was frowning at his phone, so Vi took it from him. "No," they said after a second. "We passed it a little. Not sure there is a road to it, though. Which I guess makes sense, for a nature preserve."

"Right. Direct me to the nearest spot," Nia requested. Following Vi's instructions, she brought them down a narrow residential street that ended just shy of a wide swathe of trees. "Guess that's as far as we're going."

Shutting off the car, she stepped out and looked around. The others did as well. "Hear that?" Mateo asked after a second. They all nodded. There was a high-pitched buzzing somewhere nearby. "The mosquitos they said?"

But both Andy and Vi were already shaking their heads. "That's no insect," Vi replied. "That's a drone."

"So somebody's poking around in the nature preserve," Nia stated. "No wonder they didn't want any eyes on them." She grinned. "So let's go see what they're hiding."

Nobody argued as Nia marched across the grass and into the trees and bushes beyond. Though Andy did spare a glance back at the Sienna they were leaving at the curb. "Sure hope nothing happens to it while we're gone," he muttered.

Still, it was probably a little late to worry about that now.

CHAPTER FOURTEEN

Trudging through the brush sounded incredibly loud to Vi, and they kept urging their friends to be quiet. "Not much chance of that," Nia replied from up ahead. "Sorry, none of us are exactly forest ninja."

"Eh, don't worry so much," Andy suggested with an easy shrug. "That drone's making so much noise, nobody'll hear us anyway."

Which might actually be true. The farther they went into the preserve, the louder the drone became, until it was almost deafening.

They were doing their best to head straight north, toward the uppermost edge. When Mateo, who was in front, spotted water through the trees, he slowed to a stop. "I think we're almost out of trees," he whispered as the others gathered around him. "Let's take a look."

All four of them crept forward, pushing aside branches and leaves to peer out. Sure enough, they saw water up ahead, a narrow channel of it with land easily visible on the other side. More interestingly, they saw a pair of men by the shore, both of them bent over something in the man on the left's hands. Whatever it was, it wasn't very big.

"That's Mr. Rogers," Vi said quietly. "And isn't that the guy he was talking to yesterday?"

Mateo nodded. "The former mayor, yeah. Graham something. But what've they got there?"

Andy craned his neck, leaning in for a better look. "I think it's a Gameboy," he offered. "Something with a screen, anyway. So, what, they came out here to play video games? Ooh, maybe they're pirating them!"

Nia gave him a look. "Why would they come all the way out here for that?" she demanded. "Or go through this whole charade?"

"Are we even sure it was them?" Mateo asked, mainly for form's sake. Still, there wasn't any sign of an Oscar out here, real or fake.

"We need to find out what they're doing," Vi reminded the others. "You three stay here. I'll see if I can get any closer."

Andy backed up to make room—and tripped over a root. "Aah!" he cried out as he fell, limbs flailing. "Help, the ship's going down!"

The others grabbed at him—Vi and Mateo for his arms, Nia to cover his mouth—but it was too late. Andy hit the ground with a thunderous crash.

"Who's there?" they all heard a man shout from the shore. "Come out of there at once!"

"You'd better come out, whoever you are," the second man agreed. "Don't make us come in after you."

The foursome hesitated—and suddenly a large hand reached through the bushes and latched onto Vi's arm! "Help!" they screamed, thrashing, but their assailant was too strong. Vi continued to wail as whoever it was hauled them out of the foliage.

"Vi!" Mateo charged after them, as did Nia and Andy, who'd regained his feet. In a second they were clear of the bushes and standing by the shore—facing off against Graham Jeffries and Craig Rogers. The former had Vi by the shoulders, preventing them from breaking free.

"You made a turtle the other day!" Craig said to Vi. "A nice one, too."

Graham was glaring at Mateo. "And you were at the organizers' tent, asking questions. Who the hell are you kids?"

"Just some people passing through who stopped for the festival," Nia answered, keeping her cool. "Sorry we interrupted whatever you're doing, we'll just go and leave you to it."

But the former mayor shook his head. "Too late for that now. Guess you'll have to stick around." He glanced at his compatriot. "Craig, go get the rope."

"What?" the other man stared at him. "Uncle Graham, come on, they're just kids! They're not gonna say anything."

"I'm not taking that chance!" Graham snapped. "We've waited too long and worked too hard for this! Tie them up, and do it now!"

Mateo stepped forward, as did Andy. "There's four of us and two of you," he pointed out. "And we're a whole lot younger."

"That's right," Andy said, nodding. "We're scrappy."

Graham sneered—and pulled out a gun. "You're not gonna get any older, you don't behave," he warned, aiming the weapon at Vi, who'd gone completely still at the sight of it. "Starting with this one."

The others had frozen in place as well. "Okay, let's not do anything stupid," Nia said carefully, in a calm, even tone. "Nobody has to get hurt."

Craig nodded. He looked as alarmed as the kids. "What're you doing with that?" he asked his partner—his uncle, he'd said before. "You didn't say anything about a gun! Isn't that from your Army days?"

"That's right, but believe me, it still works just fine. I brought it just in case," his uncle said with a smug look. "Good thing, too. Now tie them up and let's get on with it. Sunset'll be here before you know it."

The teacher looked like he wanted to argue, but after a few seconds he gave up. "Just do what he says, okay?" he told the kids. "Please." Then he disappeared into the woods of the preserve. The crack of branches getting softer indicated his progress.

"Sit down there," Graham instructed, indicating a sandy stretch back from the water. He let go of Vi so they could rejoin their friends.

Craig returned a few minutes later and set to work tying each of the foursome's hands and feet. "I'm really sorry about this," he said as he worked. "Nobody was supposed to even know."

"Know what?" Vi asked. "You might as well tell us now, since you're already holding us captive." They still looked a little pale, but the others were glad to see they'd recovered most of their usual pluck.

Craig hesitated, glancing back at his uncle. "We'll go first," Mateo offered. "We know you've been masquerading as the Beast of Busco. We almost caught you at it last night, but you got away."

"Yeah, and you made the pieces with your 3-D printer, right?" Nia put in. "Just like the little ones for the crafts tent."

Andy joined the conversation. "You were getting everybody over to Blue Lake so nobody could see what you two were up to out here." He tilted his head. "But what *are* you up to? What's so important you'd go to all this trouble?"

Graham, still standing back and keeping the gun on them, snorted. "What's so important? Just a fortune in buried treasure, that's what!"

"Buried treasure?" The four friends looked at each other. "Okay, that's a new one," Mateo admitted.

"That's because you're not from around here," Craig told him, finishing his ropework and standing to rejoin his uncle, who finally lowered the gun. "If you were, you'd know the story of Jim Genna."

But Vi actually nodded. "He was a gangster, right?" they asked. "Had some kind of stash up in Marshal County?" When both men stared, they shrugged. "I've got a good memory."

"Well, you're spot on," Craig replied, his tone smoothing out into what Vi recognized from before as his teacher-mode. "Vincenzo 'James' Genna was the head of the Genna crime family, up in Chicago. A rival gang ran them out of town in the 1920s. Genna died a few years later, in 1931, in Calumet City. But rumor was, back in his heyday he buried a steel box full of money somewhere out here in Indiana."

"And you think you've found it," Nia asked. "Here, by Tippecanoe Lake." She glanced at the device the two men had set aside when they'd caught them snooping. "That's for your drone, isn't it? That's how you were searching for the box."

"Ground-penetrating radar!" Vi all but shouted, then looked embarrassed at their outburst. "Sorry. But that's it, isn't it? You've got a big drone with a radar unit, and you've been using that to scan the area for this box." They frowned. "Why here, though? Is this even the right county?"

Graham laughed. "This isn't Marshal County, no. But I had a hunch. Nobody's been able to find the treasure in all this time, even though everybody said it was right off State Road Six, near Bremen. But what if it wasn't there anymore? I was in the Engineer Corps, back in the service. Saw all kinds of things wind up where they weren't supposed to. So that got me to thinking. What if there was an underground stream that washed away the dirt and soil all around it, and sent the box floating downstream a ways? Down toward Churubusco."

Vi nodded. "And Tippecanoe is the oldest, deepest, coldest lake around. If anything in the area's being fed by underground streams, it's here."

The former mayor actually gave her an approving nod. "That's right. So we've been searching and searching. But with Turtle Days coming up, we had to make sure nobody was around to see what we were doing. That's why I had Craig put together an Oscar costume and go stomping about over at Blue Lake."

He was starting to scowl again, no doubt on the verge of remembering that *they* had interrupted things, so Andy asked quickly, "Did you find it?"

That brought a satisfied smirk to the older man's face. "Did we ever!" He frowned. "It's buried too deep for us to just dig out, though."

Now his grin looked a little dangerous. "But that's okay. We came up with a Plan B."

Next to him, his nephew frowned. "I'm still not sure about all this, uncle."

But Graham waved that off. "We've come too far to quit now," he reminded Craig. "Just a few more hours, and it'll all be over."

The foursome looked at each other. A few hours? What happened then? Because "it'll all be over" had a pretty ominous ring to it!

Chapter Fifteen

The two men moved away, huddling over the drone's controller—and over a large box set off to one side, with the word "Property U.S. Army" stenciled in faded letters on one side. That at least gave the four friends time to huddle together and talk, keeping their voices down.

"So," Nia started. "Whose idea was visiting this 'quaint little town fair,' again?" She was glaring at Mateo, though he knew her anger was more at their predicament than at him. Still, he shrugged apologetically.

"Hey, the fair itself *is* fun," he pointed out. "And, honestly, this whole little mystery about the Beast has been, too." He glanced down at his feet, bound and stretched out in front of him. "It's just this last part that sucks."

"So what do we do about it?" Vi asked. "Because I don't know about you, but I'm not keen on waiting to see what they've got planned for us once they're done with whatever the hell they're doing right now."

Andy shrugged—except he did it with his whole body, contorting his entire right side like he was suddenly hunchbacked. His face was all twisted up as well, and at first the others thought he might be having a seizure or something. But then he gave a sigh of relief. "Got it!" And he shifted sideways a little so they could see the small, red globe clutched between his fingers.

"A cherry bomb?" Nia asked. "And what exactly're you gonna do with that, hm? Blow the ropes to bits?"

But this time he would not be dissuaded by her snark. "Nope," he answered loftily instead. "I'm going to toss it in their midst and, while they're distracted, we'll make our escape."

"Their midst?" Mateo repeated. "First off, there's only two of them. Second, since when do you use words like 'midst'?"

Andy looked slightly wounded by that. "I can use big words," he countered. "Or fancy ones. Or whatever. And I meant what I said. I throw this, it goes off, they're surprised, we run. Simple."

"You're forgetting the part where our feet are tied," Vi pointed out.

Nia nodded. "And the part where you need fire to set that off."

"And the part where your hands are tied behind your back, they're a good ten feet away, and you're a terrible shot," Mateo chimed in. "Sorry."

Andy glared at his three friends. "Well, have any of you got a better idea? Because it's getting dark, and that means we're running out of time."

None of them did. "Could you light it with friction?" Vi asked. "You know, scrape it against a rock to get a spark?"

He felt beneath him with his other hand. "Maybe, but I don't have any rocks," he answered. "Anybody got one?"

Nia shook her head. So did Vi. Mateo started to—then stopped. "Hang on. I might have something better." He fumbled at his pants pocket, but couldn't get his hands far enough around to reach properly. "Nia, help me out here."

She glared at him. "If this is some kinda weird come-on…"

"It's not!" he promised. "Swear!"

"Fine." She twisted until she was facing Vi, her back to Mateo, and then felt around, her fingers grazing his leg and then inching their way up the seam of his jeans to his pocket. Then they dipped in—and, after a moment, pulled out a long, slim metal shape.

"Okay," she asked, craning her neck to see what she'd found. "Why do you have a nail file in your pocket and I don't?"

Mateo shrugged. "I take better care of my nails than you do. People notice that sort of thing." He jerked his chin toward Andy. "Give it to him. He can use it to get a spark."

"Against what?" Andy asked, but Vi had brightened. They went through similar contortions to his own earlier ones, and with a triumphant little snort produced a metal pen. "Ta-da!"

"Nice!" Andy accepted both implements, almost dropping each one at least once. He tried to get them into position over the cherry bomb, but juggling all three was next to impossible, especially with his hands tied behind his back. "A little help, maybe?"

Vi sighed and turned away from him, thrusting out their own hands. "Give me the pen and the file." He passed them along, and they grasped one in each hand. "You ready?"

Andy shifted, bringing the little firecracker up until it brushed Vi's hands. "Ready."

"Right." They scraped the two items together with a loud screech. Fortunately, Craig and his uncle didn't notice. "Anything?"

Nia had positioned herself to watch the process, while Mateo served as a lookout. "Nope. Try again."

Vi scraped again. "There was a spark!" Nia reported. "A little one, but still!"

"Might want to hurry," Mateo remarked. "They're digging around in that box and… I think they've got dynamite."

All efforts paused as four sets of eyes turned to stare at the two men. Who were now holding long reddish-brown sticks with wicks at one end.

"Um, that's just a prop, right?" Andy called. "To scare the money out of hiding?"

Graham laughed. It was not a pleasant sound. "It's real, all right," he replied. "Another little souvenir from my Army days. Used a few sticks over the years to blow up stumps or take out walls, but I reckon we've still got enough to get the job done."

"You're going to blow up… what, exactly?" Vi asked. "The river?"

"A part of the bank," Craig told them. "Right where the treasure's buried. Blast out a big enough hole that we can pretty much just reach in and grab it."

"Now, hush," Graham warned. "Or I'll drag you four over on top of it." His nephew looked horrified, but the foursome didn't need any additional urging to leave the two men alone and return to their own efforts instead.

"Even if this works," Nia pointed out, "How're we gonna get free? Or at least enough to run?"

Mateo grinned at her. "Been working on that," he answered. "Mr. Rogers might be great at science and at 3-D printing, but he sucks at knots. I, on the other hand, was an Eagle Scout. I've just about got my hands free."

"So maybe we should wait until we're untied, then set this thing off?" Vi asked. "It'd be a helluva lot easier!"

But Andy shook his head. "No time. We do this, you take care of that." That made sense, and Vi got back to work at setting off sparks.

It took another three tries, but finally a spark from the pen and file caught the end of the cherry bomb's little fuse. "It's lit!" Nia reported.

"Give it here!" Mateo urged—holding out an untied hand! Andy quickly bobbled the lit firecracker to him. Mateo turned, sighting on the two men, who were crouched down by the water's edge. He squinted. He drew back his arm.

And he lobbed the cherry bomb in a perfect arc, landing it right between them.

Graham reacted first, glancing up and over at them in utter horror. "No!" He staggered to his feet, his nephew right behind him. "You idiots!" the former mayor shouted as he stumbled away.

Then the dynamite blew. The firecracker had caught on the explosives' fuse, setting them off early.

It was like being hit in the face and chest with a tremendous punch of hot air. The kids all fell backward, slammed to the ground by the blast. Graham and Craig were tossed into the air, hitting the earth heavily several feet away. The entire riverbank shook.

And a part of it slid into the water, disappearing without a sound.

"Damn you!" Graham was screaming, though they could barely hear him through the ringing in their ears. "If that treasure slips away because of you…"

Craig had managed to regain his feet. "Come on," he urged, grabbing his uncle's arm and tugging him back toward the rest of their gear. "We can check." His voice sounded faint, and he was shaking.

The two men shambled over to their equipment, giving the foursome a chance to collect themselves. "Everybody okay?" Mateo asked.

The others nodded.

"Great. Hold still." Nia was closest, so he untied her hands first. "Help Andy." Mateo untied his own feet, then crawled to Vi and undid the knots binding them. "Good?"

They stood, slowly and with a few winces. "Good."

In a minute, they were all on their feet, leaning against each other for support. "This is like being drunk, only without the fun part first," Andy remarked. When Vi cocked an eyebrow, he added, "or so I've heard."

Just then, one of the men let out a whoop. It was Graham. "Yes!" he shouted, taking a few unsteady steps toward the new shoreline. "It worked!"

Craig was right behind him, the teacher pulling on a pair of heavy leather work gloves. "I got this," he assured his uncle, brushing past him and crouching down. He extended his arms, leaning forward, and grasped something the foursome could not see.

Graham, however, turned back toward them, an ugly expression on his face. "We were gonna let you go," he told them, though his words sounded hollow. "After we had it. No reason to keep you, nothing you could do to stop us. But you nearly blew us up! And almost cost us the treasure!" It was hard to say which thought upset him more. "So the way I see it, this is your own fault." His gun hand rose slowly, the weapon rising with it.

Craig twisted back around, though he was still wrestling with whatever he'd found. "Uncle, no!" he shouted. "Don't!"

"Oh, grow a pair!" Graham snapped, not looking behind him. "You gonna let a buncha kids ruin this for us?"

"We can just let them go, like you said," Craig argued. "So what if they saw? We'll have the money, and that's that."

But his uncle was still glowering at them. "No," he said flatly. "It's gotta be done." He leveled the gun at Mateo, who tensed with some crazy notion of dodging the bullet about to come his way.

Which was when the ground moved again. Only, this time, there wasn't any dynamite.

"What the hell?" Graham demanded, stumbling and almost toppling over. It was like an earthquake, but the friends could see that the other bank was unaffected. Same with the area beyond their little clearing. The earth was only shifting right here.

Shifting—and rising. As something emerged from it.

Something large and angular, sand and dirt sloughing off hard ridges.

"Is that...?" Andy whispered, as the shape continued to lift up. It was now nearly as high as his head, and considerably wider, broadening out even further behind. The front part was the narrowest, ending in almost a point, and just below that was a triangular opening.

When the first massive, clawed foot emerged, they knew.

The last of the dirt fell away from the head, revealing the hooked beak mouth and the large, round red eyes in all their glory.

"It's Oscar!" Vi breathed.

The Beast of Busco hissed at them all—but its eyes were fixed on Graham as the former mayor stared up at it in sheer terror.

When the colossal turtle lunged forward, Mateo grabbed his friends' hands. "Run!"

And they did, not looking back as Oscar unleashed all his pent-up fury on their former captors.

Chapter Sixteen

"Go go go!" Andy chanted, his long legs propelling him forward and his extreme flexibility letting him weave between the trees and bushes without needing to slow down. Mateo had a decent amount of strength and agility, but Nia easily bested him, her dancer's legs pistoning as she dove through the foliage like it was a crowd of New Yorkers trying to push their way onto the train. It was Vi who had the most trouble, being the shortest and lacking some of the same muscle. But what they didn't have in power they made up for in stamina, and by the time the four of them broke through the trees and saw manicured lawns, streets, houses, and the ever-faithful Toyota Sienna still waiting for them, they were the only one not panting like they'd just run a marathon.

Or tried to outrun both a pair of potentially murderous thieves and an enormous, pissed off mythical creature.

"You all saw that, right?" Andy asked, gasping, as they piled into the minivan, slamming the doors shut the second they were inside. Nia had the car in gear almost before they'd buckled in and peeled out of the little housing development like — well, like Oscar might come barreling after them at any second.

"I mean," he tried again once he'd recovered some breath and was no longer afraid of being crushed by the car's acceleration. "That wasn't just me, right? You all saw it? The freaking Beast of Busco?"

"We saw it," Mateo agreed from the front passenger seat. "Not sure what we saw, but we definitely saw it."

"Deus ex machina," Vi put in, and the others all nodded. As theater kids, they were all well familiar with the term. "I mean, it did pretty much come out of nowhere and save our collective butts."

"Yeah, but how?" Nia asked, eyes on the road she was currently racing down. "This isn't a play, so it had to come from somewhere. And why now? Why us?"

But Vi had been thinking about that. "Not us," they corrected, gathering steam as their thoughts came together. "And not nowhere, really. It came from underneath." When none of the others responded, they sighed. "Didn't any of you do the reading?" That, at least, drew a chuckle and a wince at thoughts of the many assignments they'd shared over the last semester. "Alligator snapping turtles need to stay almost or even completely submerged most of the time. Their skin dries out, otherwise. And alligator snapping turtles, they feed by laying on the bottom of a river or lake and opening their mouth wide, then just waiting for fish and eels and whatever else to come wandering in."

Andy rubbed at his eyes. "Um, why would anything, even a fish, be dumb enough to do that?"

Vi smiled, pleased at being able to show off their hard-won knowledge. "Because their tongues have this little appendage that looks just like a wriggling worm. They lay there, half-buried in mud, and fish and stuff see the worm, go to eat it, and—bam!" They slammed their hands together, making the other three jump. "It eats them instead."

"So you're saying Oscar was buried in Tippecanoe Lake for, what, seventy, eighty years?" Mateo asked. He shook his head. "Man, I'd get bored after a day!"

"Alligator snapping turtles can live into their hundreds," Vi reminded. "And they get bigger with each year of their lives. He'd have needed someplace that deep to stay submerged." They frowned. "Though I wonder if maybe he got stuck."

"Until Graham and Craig blasted the riverbank to smithereens," Nia commented. "And set him loose."

"So just really good timing," Andy offered. He sighed. "Too bad, I kinda liked the idea of a gift from the gods."

"Mysterious ways and all that," Mateo said, throwing a smile back at his friend. Then he turned serious. "Speaking of ways, what do we do now? Any thoughts, gang?"

Nia nodded. "Go to the marshal," she declared unequivocally. "Tell her what happened. She can arrest them."

"For what, exactly?" Vi asked. "They're not really stealing, are they? Not if this guy's been dead for almost a century. Using the dynamite, maybe, but I feel like that'd just get them a fine and a slap on the wrist."

"What about kidnapping?" Nia asked fiercely, glaring at the road. But her eyes darted to the rearview in time to see Vi shake their head.

"It's our word against theirs," they pointed out. "And they're well known around here. We're strangers. Besides which, is it really kidnapping? They didn't take us anywhere. They just tied us up for a bit." They held up their hands to forestall the angry response they could see building in Nia's head. "I'm not saying it wasn't wrong, and that they shouldn't be punished. I'm just not sure what the marshal can do about it."

"Well, what do you suggest?" Mateo asked, speaking calmly to soothe Nia's ire. "How do we get back at them?"

"Feed them to Oscar?" Andy offered, which got a snort from the others.

"How about we take what they were after?" Nia suggested after a moment. "They did all this for that money, right? What if we steal it back from them? We could donate it to a charity or something. Or give it to the Turtle Days people. Whatever, as long as they came out emptyhanded."

Mateo scratched his chin. "That might actually work," he agreed. "It's not like they have any more claim to it than we do, so they can't really accuse us of stealing. There's just one problem." He twisted around in his seat to peer toward the back. "They're back there somewhere, and we're out here, and getting farther away by the minute."

Which was when an enormous, car-sized turtle came hurtling out of a side road and nearly slammed right into them.

"Whoa!" Nia spun the wheel, sending the Sienna skipping to the side so rapidly it rose on its two side wheels, spurting along that way for a minute before the other set slammed back onto the ground. "What the hell!" The giant turtle rocketed past them without even slowing down.

"Oscar's come to eat us after all!" Andy wailed, covering his face with his hands. But Vi, who had been staring out the window in rapt fascination as much as terror, gave a startled little laugh and reached for his hand.

"It isn't Oscar," they told the others. "Look."

Now that it was ahead of them, their headlights could pick it up—and now that they were no longer afraid of being run over, or eaten, they could look properly.

Only, what they saw didn't seem to make much sense.

"Is it... a car?" Mateo said. "I think it's a car, right? Those are taillights, aren't they?"

Vi nodded. "It's a car. A VW Beetle, I think. Only it's been made up to look like a giant alligator snapping turtle." They frowned. "It's really good, actually. They put a skin over the top to look like a shell and built up or replaced the hood to look like the turtle's head. I'd need to see it again, but I think they may've used refractors to channel the headlights through the eyes."

"Okay, so it's a marvel of engineering," Andy agreed, a bit snappishly as he was somewhat embarrassed by his earlier outcry. "What the hell's it doing all the way out here?"

But Mateo had an answer to that. "I caught a glimpse of the driver," he said. "It was Craig. I guess he's got a car as well as that blue pickup. So, more of the whole 'the Beast is real' charade?"

Nia smirked. "Naw, I see what they're doing. Look, they wanted to wait on the explosives until dark, right? Because what happens at dark tonight?" The others all shrugged. "The fireworks!"

"Right!" Mateo said, snapping his fingers. "Cindy wanted me to meet her for them. And after that comes the parade awards, she said. Where they bring all the floats back together. So they made themselves a float!"

Vi nodded. "And that way, when someone finds out about what happened at Tippecanoe, nobody'll suspect them. Seeing their float there with the rest, everybody'll assume they were in the parade this morning, and at the festival the whole time."

"Yeah." Nia grinned, sharp-toothed and eager, a bit like a predator herself. "Unless we run them off the road before they can reach the festival."

The others yelped, flung back in their seats as she gunned the engine and the Sienna shot forward, chasing the giant turtle into the night.

Chapter Seventeen

Vi found their breath—and their voice—first. "Uh, Nia?" They called from the back seat. "You're not seriously planning on running them down, right?"

Nia just chuckled, not bothering to shift her gaze from the green blur zipping along up ahead and growing steadily larger.

Andy leaned forward. "Nia? Hey, you can't hit their car, okay? Remember, we have to deliver the Sienna in one piece. Undamaged. Or my uncle'll take it out of my hide."

"Oh, relax," she replied absently. "It'll be fine. Mostly."

Andy threw a concerned look at Mateo, who shrugged and held up his hands. "Big help you are," Andy muttered.

The turtle-car was closer now, close enough that they could make out the rear window, cleverly concealed within the fake shell. Nia hit the horn, making the other three jump.

"So, not going for stealth, then?" Mateo joked as she honked again.

She shook her head. "They already know we're here. Now they're gonna feel it." Her hands were wrapped around the steering wheel and she was leaning forward like she meant to slam into the other car herself. The Sienna continued to race, narrowing the gap second by second.

They didn't see the turn until the other car suddenly swerved right—leaving nothing but fields ahead.

"Ah!" Andy shouted as he was tossed backward from Nia whipping the car around the bend, tires screeching the whole way. "Nia, stop!"

"Can't," she all but panted back. "They're getting away." The little car didn't have as big an engine, but they'd known the turn was coming and had handled it better, putting some distance between the two vehicles in the process.

Mateo had shifted his own focus to peer out ahead, into the night. He squinted at what he saw. "Intersection up ahead," he reported after a second.

Vi had hauled out their phone and pulled up the map app. "That should be 450," they called out. "That leads back to town. It's the way we came."

"On it," Nia answered. And, a moment later when the turtle-car took a sharp left, she was right behind them, regaining their earlier proximity.

"Nia," Andy said, clutching the back of her seat. "I'm serious, you can't scratch the car."

She snarled and waved him off, but he persisted. "The only reason he let us drive it is we promised it'd be pristine when it arrived," he reminded her. "If it's not, we're screwed."

"They tried to kill us!" she snapped. "They can't just get away with that!"

Andy shifted and carefully, tentatively, placed his hand on Nia's shoulder. "They won't," he promised. "But you can't hit them. Besides, what if somebody got hurt? Even if they're jerks, do you really wanna be responsible for that? And what if it was one of us, instead?"

That made her scowl—but lift her foot slightly where it had been pressing the accelerator to the floor. The Sienna was still moving at breakneck speeds, but slowly, gradually, the space between the two cars increased. "No," she admitted after a minute, her voice still tight but not as manic. "I couldn't handle that."

Andy let out the breath he'd been holding. Beside him, Vi leaned back in their own seat and gave him a thumbs-up. "So," they offered, "instead of ramming speed, we follow them back. We know where they're going, and it's not like there's anywhere to hide. Maybe they'll get stuck at a stoplight or something, and then we can think of some delay that doesn't involve a car crash."

Nia nodded. "Fine." Her jaw was still tight, teeth still clenched, but she forced herself to take slow, steady breaths, gradually easing some of that tension. "We'll play the waiting game. For now. But we'd better come up with something, because we're not letting them get away with it."

"No, we're not," Vi agreed. Nia's eyes flicked up to study her friend in the rearview—and widened. "What?"

"I—" Nia shook her head. "Sorry. Thought I saw something behind us. But there's nothing there, right?"

Both Vi and Andy twisted around to stare out the back. "Nothing," Andy confirmed after a minute. "No lights at all."

"And anybody trying this road in the dark'd have to be nuts," Mateo said as they hit another turn, onto a small state route. That then led, through a few twists, back to another road that might've been the one they'd just left. They lost sight of the turtle-car a few times, but once they'd hit the straight path again, they found it easily. Nia sped up enough to get them close—but not so close as to smash into the other car, which was something of a relief to her friends.

"Okay," Mateo said, turning sideways so he could see the others as things settled down a bit. "So we need a way to stop them from joining the other floats and then disappearing afterward. Ideas?"

Vi pondered, but finally shook their head. "Nothing comes to mind so far," they admitted. "Sorry."

Mateo nodded, his expression glum. "Yeah, me neither. Andy? Nia?"

"We can always go back to ramming them," Nia offered. But she didn't sound as bloodthirsty as she had a few minutes before.

Andy slumped, shoving his hands into his pockets—and then brightened. "What about these?" he asked, pulling the rest of the cherry bombs free and holding them up. "Worked once, right?"

"That's..." Mateo started to say, but trailed off, a grin shaping up instead. "That actually might work."

Beside him, Nia's own smile sharpened once more. "Oh, yeah. Prepare for some explosions of your own, suckers."

Chapter Eighteen

Mateo frowned. "Okay, problem," he stated. "How're we gonna light the things? None of us smoke."

But Vi grinned and dug in their bag. "Here." They passed a cheap disposable lighter forward with a shrug. "I use it to seal threads."

"Crafting for the win," Andy said, smiling as he tossed a firecracker to Mateo. "You're a better shot," he admitted. "I'll just supply the ammo. But you know I've got you beat hands down at juggling."

His friend nodded. "No argument. Okay. Nia, can you pull up alongside them when I say so?" They'd just taken a soft right and were now traveling along Route 33 — which they knew turned into Main Street once it hit Churubusco. Time was running out.

She smirked in response. "Just watch me." And nudged the gas enough to close the distance down to almost spitting range.

They were passing a small cluster of shops and businesses, including a school, a garage, and a gas station, so Mateo held off. A few minutes later, they'd left all of those behind and had nothing but farmland on either side. The road was clear except for them and the villains in the turtle-car just up ahead, though twice Nia thought she saw a flicker of movement in the rearview.

"Okay," Mateo said, rolling down his window. He flicked the lighter and readied the cherry bomb next to the tiny flame. "Now!"

Nia jerked the wheel, sending the Sienna hurtling into the opposite lane, and sped up at the same time. They were beside the turtle car in seconds, then passing it. "Keep going!" Mateo shouted — and tossed the lit firecracker just in front of the disguised Beetle.

They zoomed on past, and were now in front of the other car, swerving back into that lane.

Then the firecracker went off.

It sounded like a gunshot. And, the way Craig swerved, he must have thought so, too. The smaller vehicle careened wildly, slewing across both lanes. Fortunately, there wasn't anyone else on the road.

Unfortunately, the high school science teacher proved to be a decent driver, and quickly regained control of his car. They had fallen slightly behind the Sienna but showed no signs of stopping.

"Try again," Andy urged, handing over another from his dwindling supply. Mateo complied, this time just lobbing the cherry bomb backward so it fell behind them and went off immediately in front of the Beetle's fabricated turtle head.

Craig only swerved a little this time and didn't even slow down.

"No good," Mateo reported, closing his window and handing the lighter back to Vi. "He knows they're not a real threat."

"We could just hit the brakes," Nia offered. "Yes, I know it might scratch the precious minivan, but this thing's tough. And he's too close to avoid us. That'd put a stop to them."

But Vi shook their head. "What if it didn't, though? That head is either rubber or plastic, it could act like an enormous front bumper, take all the impact. And if their car stayed running and ours didn't, we'd have no way to even catch up again."

They all considered that—and broke out in various groans and gasps as a now-familiar sign zipped by on the right: "Blue Lake Campground."

They were almost out of time.

Nia started swerving, back and forth across the center line. "What're you doing?" Andy asked, clinging to his seatbelt and the strap above his seat.

"Making them hang back a little," she answered. "They've got to keep some distance in case I do hit the brakes." She shrugged. "Buys us a few extra seconds."

But Mateo had seen another sign approaching. "Not enough." And there, looming up ahead, was a copy of the same banner they'd seen when first approaching town a few days before: "Welcome to Churubusco. Turtle Town, USA."

Vi snorted at the cartoon turtle displayed there. "That looks nothing like him."

"Artist's prerogative," Andy suggested. "He's not exactly photogenic."

They giggled but gave up any further reply as houses and shops began to spring up on either side. They'd reached town.

"And there's the festival," Mateo said, pointing ahead. Sure enough, only a few blocks in front of them was a crowd, gathered on either side of Main Street. With a row of floats lined up across the road itself.

Behind them, they heard a horn. Craig and Graham had seen the event as well. They knew in a few minutes they'd be home free.

"It's now or never," Nia declared, and spun the wheel, slamming on the brakes as she did. The Sienna slid sideways and came to a stop across the lanes, blocking the road completely.

The turtle-car honked and kept on coming.

"They're gonna ram us!" Mateo shouted, clutching the dashboard.

"Get ready!" Vi yelled.

"Brace for impact!" Nia urged.

"Not the car!" Andy screamed.

They could see the two men in the other car now. Craig looked scared, Graham resolute.

The turtle-car was nearly upon them.

And then a massive shape rose up behind them.

The foursome heard a loud hiss, then a terrible rending sound.

And the turtle-car was flung to the side.

It crashed into a lamppost, which came down upon its roof, smashing that in.

Behind it, the real Beast of Busco roared his challenge.

The car lurched forward, and Oscar swatted it back with one massive, clawed foot. He tore jagged gaps into the driver's door, denting it badly. The car slammed into the curb, teetering back on its right wheels—and toppled over.

Oscar screamed at it.

Other screams rose from nearby. The crowd had seen him!

Alarmed by all the sudden noise, the giant turtle took one look at all the people. Then—with a single quick glance at the Sienna and the four people staring back at it—it turned and fled. Within seconds, it had vanished into the night.

"Wow." That was Vi. "Do you think it recognized us from the lake?"

"It sure recognized Graham and Craig," Mateo answered. "And not in a good way."

Nia pounded the steering wheel, but not in anger. "I knew I saw something behind us! It must have been following them, too!"

Andy nodded. "Yeah, I don't think it liked their car's decorations much. Must've seen that as an insult or something."

"Whatever the reason, it did what we couldn't," Vi pointed out. "They didn't make it to the other floats, and nobody's gonna forget it." They slid the side door open and hopped out. "Come on. Time to finish this."

The others unbuckled and followed, making their way toward the mangled turtle-car still flipped on its side. Its wheels spun lazily, but of course it wasn't going anywhere.

Just like a real turtle.

Chapter Nineteen

As they approached the downed car, a tall, dark-skinned woman in a police uniform pushed through the crowd. "What the hell is going on here?" Marshal Cohn demanded, stomping toward them, her deputy right behind her. She had one hand resting on her gun, the gang noticed, but at least it was still in its holster.

Nia stepped forward to meet the officer. "Sorry for disrupting the awards ceremony," she announced, making sure her voice carried to the attendees gathering ever closer. "But this was important." She gestured toward the car, and the two men struggling to pull themselves out through the shattered driver's side window. "Graham Jeffries and Craig Rogers have been faking all those recent sightings of the Beast of Busco." There were gasps of outrage from the crowd.

"But they weren't doing it just for fun," Mateo put in as the two officers reached them. "Or to drum up more interest in Turtle Days. They had a more immediate goal in mind."

Andy nodded. "Yeah, they were drawing people to Blue Lake to keep everyone away from Tippecanoe Lake—and the treasure they'd found there."

Vi took up the narrative. "It's Jim Genna's lost treasure," they explained. "Graham figured out it had washed down to Tippecanoe. They found it but had to blow up part of the preserve there to get it out."

"They were using the fireworks to cover up the noise," Nia resumed. "And then they were gonna sneak back into the festival alongside the other floats, so nobody'd ever know it was them."

Mateo grinned. "Only, they got more than they'd bargained for."

"Yeah." Vi laughed. "Like the real Beast of Busco. He wasn't too happy with them disturbing his nap."

"We chased them, and he did too," Andy agreed. "You all saw it." The crowd cheered, and he took a bow.

Cohn was studying the four of them. "That's quite a story," she said. "I assume you can back it up?"

Vi nodded. "You'll find the rest of their gear still back at the preserve. And the treasure should be there, in their car."

The marshal turned and, with a few long strides, had reached the turtle-car. There she helped a dazed Craig and Graham extricate themselves—and took a glance in the back seat. "Big metal box there, covered in rust and mud," she declared. "Care to explain what that might be, and where it came from?"

"It's ours!" Graham managed, trying to twist free, but she had his arm in a vice-like grip. "You can't have it!"

"We'll see," Cohn replied sharply. "If it really did come from the preserve, it doesn't belong to you. And if you did blow up part of that stretch to get it, well, that land's protected. You're looking at federal charges, most likely."

Craig hung his head. "I'm sorry," he said. "We weren't looking to hurt anyone, or anything. Uncle Graham said it was just there for the taking!"

His uncle glared at him. "Shut it, you!"

Cohn sighed and shook her head, tugging a set of handcuffs off her belt and gesturing for her deputy to do the same. "You're both under arrest for disturbing the peace, trespassing, destruction of protected property, and probably some other things that'll turn up later. Read 'em their rights and get 'em out of here."

"This would have worked, if not for you blasted kids!" Graham shouted at the foursome as he and his nephew were being led away. "You and that bloody Beast!"

Watching him go for a second, the marshal shook her head, then turned back toward the four friends. "Looks like we might owe you some thanks," she said slowly, the hints of a smile tugging at her lips. "Not least of which for bringing Oscar back to life."

"Oh, not sure that was—" Andy started, but Vi elbowed him in the side and he shut up.

"Our pleasure," Vi said over his sputtering. "I bet you're gonna have a lot more sightings in future."

The others all nodded, and now the marshal did smile. "Yeah, could make things pretty exciting around here. But for now, I think there's a festival that needs to get going again. Y'all gonna stick around for it?"

They exchanged glances and then all nodded. "Wouldn't miss it," Mateo agreed, having just spotted a smiling Cindy in the crowd.

"Here we go," Andy muttered as the marshal sauntered off and Mateo detached himself a few steps behind.

Nia hip-checked him. "Eh, you had fun. And we've got one hell of a story to tell. For now, though, you know what I think?" She glanced at the Sienna, still blocking the street — and at the party starting up just beyond it. "I think we earned ourselves some fun. You coming?" And she headed for the crowd.

"Heck, yeah!" Andy shouted, any misgivings forgotten.

Vi was right behind but paused a second to glance back at the way out of town. Was it their imagination, or did they catch just a glimpse of big red eyes and a hooked mouth watching them from the shadows? "Thank you," they whispered. "And I'm glad we met."

Then they were hurrying after their friends, and toward the end of a town-wide celebration that had just been given new life.

ABOUT THE AUTHOR

Aaron Rosenberg is the best-selling, award-winning author of over fifty novels, including the Twin Cities Cryptids urban fantasy/cozy series, the DuckBob SF comedy series, the Relicant Chronicles epic fantasy series, the Areyat Islands fantasy pirate mystery series, the upcoming BEO Files urban fantasy series, and, with David Niall Wilson, the *O.C.L.T.* occult thriller series. His tie-in work contains novels for *Star Trek*, *Warhammer*, *World of WarCraft*, *Stargate: Atlantis*, *Shadowrun*, *Mutants & Masterminds*, and *Eureka* and short stories for *The X-Files*, *World of Darkness*, *Crusader Kings II*, *Deadlands*, *Master of Orion*, and *Europa Universalis IV*. He has written children's books (including the original series STEM Squad and Pete and Penny's Pizza Puzzles, the award-winning *Bandslam: The Junior Novel* and the #1 best-selling *42: The Jackie Robinson Story*), educational books, and roleplaying games (including the original games *Asylum*, *Spookshow*, and *Chosen*; work for White Wolf, Wizards of the Coast, Fantasy Flight, Pinnacle, and many others; the Origins Award-winning *Gamemastering Secrets*; and the Gold ENnie-winning *Lure of the Lich Lord*). He is a founding member of Crazy 8 Press. Aaron lives in New York with his family.

You can follow him online at gryphonrose.com, on Facebook at facebook.com/gryphonrose, on BSky at @gryphonrose.bsky.social, on Instagram at the_gryphonrose, and on X (formerly known as Twitter) @gryphonrose.

About the Artist

Until his decades-long disappearance, JW Harp was known for his trippy underground comic strip *Captain Thetan*, about a seafarer who controls reality for himself and others. This otherworldly character appeared in a dozen issues of the classic rare underground zine *Sandanista Romp*. JW has reemerged thanks largely to eSpec Books' Systema Paradoxa series. In 2023, JW started Skilletfire Studios with comic-book author Scott Eckelaert. Under the Skilletfire Studios mantle, JW has produced the graphic novel *Boylon Heights*, and the *Gimme Five Comics* series. Since its launch, *Gimme Five Comics* has included work by Artyom Topilin, Elena Cerisciola, John L. French, Keith Lansdale, and Joe R. Lansdale with more to come.

JW grew up in the seedy parts of South Carolina, which is all of it. He feels part Canadian and part Costa Rican these days. He lives in North Carolina. Please get in touch with him at jwharp@skilletfire.com.

artist's rendition of the Beast of Busco

The Beast of Busco

(Also Known as Oscar)

Origins: In 1898, near Churubusco, Indiana, a local farmer reported sighting a giant turtle in the lake on his farm. No further note was taken on the matter until fifty years later when two local men went fishing on the lake and likewise reported sighting the turtle, estimating it to be at least five hundred pounds, larger than any known specimen.

Description: Said to be longer than ten feet, with a shell the size of a car top and a head as large as a child, the Beast of Busco is estimated to weigh over a quarter of a ton. Given the descriptions, the theory is that the Beast—affectionately named Oscar after the farmer who originally reported him and who owned the farm and lake it is said to call home—is a rather large specimen of alligator snapper. While this species averages forty to seventy pounds, one has been recorded at 236 pounds, and there is an unverified account of one weighing 403 pounds, documented in Kansas in 1937.

Life Cycle: alligator snappers can live up to four hundred years, gaining an estimated one pound a year. Though primarily found in warmer regions, as they age they tend to move to more northern climes, lending some faint veracity to the possibility of one making its way to Indiana.

History: First encountered in 1898, Oscar would not be sighted again until 1948 by two locals fishing in the lake he purportedly calls home. Then again, soon after, by the farmer who now owned the property.

The report was picked up by the local newspaper and somehow went national, with reporters and spectators coming in droves to witness the farmer's efforts to trap the Beast of Busco, going to more and more extreme efforts, from attempting to drain the lake to sending in a deep-sea diver and even dredging. The farmer became obsessed, devising all sorts of traps, only to have them fail. There were more sightings, however, including one in 1949 where two hundred spectators saw the turtle surface in an attempt to consume a duck being used as bait.

Though Oscar was never captured, the town embraced him as their own and celebrate his legend with a four-day event called Turtle Days each year.

Capture the Cryptids!

Cryptid Crate is a monthly subscription box filled with various cryptozoology and paranormal-themed items to wear, display, and collect. Expect a carefully curated box filled with creeptastic pieces from indie makers and artisans pertaining to bigfoot, sasquatch, UFOs, ghosts, and other cryptid and mysterious creatures (apparel, decor, media, etc).

Now Featuring Cryptid Crate Jr.!

http://CryptidCrate.com